To Clive
For a memorable
adventure
Dave N
July) Aug 2017

THE SKY TRAP

Also by D. S. Halacy, Jr.

Dive from the Sky

Earthquakes: A Natural History

The Energy Trap

Fabulous Fireball

Master Spy

The Secret of the Cove

Sky on Fire

Soaring

Weather Changers

THE
SKY
TRAP

by D. S. Halacy, Jr.

THOMAS NELSON INC., PUBLISHERS
Nashville   New York

Copyright © 1975 by D. S. Halacy, Jr.

All rights reserved under International and Pan-American Conventions. Published in Nashville, Tennessee, by Thomas Nelson Inc., Publishers, and simultaneously in Don Mills, Ontario, by Thomas Nelson & Sons (Canada) Limited. Manufactured in the United States of America.

First edition

Library of Congress Cataloging in Publication Data

Halacy, Daniel Stephen.
  The sky trap.

  SUMMARY: When he is forced to make an emergency landing in his glider plane, a teen-ager accidentally discovers the hideout of dope smugglers in Arizona.
  [1. Gliding—Fiction. 2. Smuggling—Fiction]
I. Title.
PZ7.H1282Sl   [Fic]   75-12957
ISBN 0-8407-6461-8

THE SKY TRAP

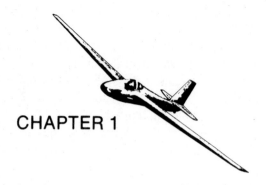

CHAPTER 1

The temperature was 103 degrees in Tucson, Arizona—hot but not unusually so for a July day. There was little wind, and the column of dust rotating like a smoky dervish moved slowly across the stretch of highway known as the Miracle Mile. Like a pale miniature tornado, the dust devil swirled sizable scraps of paper into the air, and for a moment even a tumbleweed from a nearby field spiraled upward.

A motorist, already unhappy in his uncooled vehicle, blistered the air with invectives as sand peppered his windshield, raced through the car itself, and blocked his vision so that he had to slow abruptly. Then, almost as quickly as it had formed, the corkscrewing column of hot air faded away. The well-dusted motorist watched it vanish, and wished it were winter.

Although few of those in its path knew it, the earth-bound dust devil was merely the bottom, visible portion of a still rapidly rising column of air. Fifty feet across at the bottom, it slowly broadened into a funnel shape that reached more than two miles into the hot Arizona sky. One of the few who were aware of this fact knew it because he was flying near the top of the rising column of air, or thermal, as pilots called it. And just above him was the

7

glorious end result of the furious little dust devil—a flat-bottomed, swelling white cumulus cloud a thousand feet across and still growing.

Grant Stone pushed the stick forward as the strong updraft rocketed his sailplane upward into the mist of the huge cloud. As the shrill scream of the audio variometer faded, a broad grin softened his lean face, and he relaxed in sheer joy. Some test flight! he thought. Some test flight for the fifty-foot BG-16 he had built himself from bundles of plywood and fabric, lengths of steel tubing, and sheets of plastic.

His sailplane, perhaps the last design of well-known Gus Briegleb at El Mirage, California, was officially the BG-12/16. The craft was sleeker than earlier BG's, and its smooth lines had attracted Grant the first time he saw one of them. Perhaps he should have added the letter A to the name for the further change he had made with mechanic Harry Shaughnessy's expert help. Instead of the standard fixed landing gear, they had installed a retractable wheel, plus the fiberglass doors that smoothly enclosed it.

"Just two things to remember," Harry had warned Grant. "Remember to put it up, and you'll fly a little faster. Remember to put it down, and your landings will be quieter."

As the sleek white craft fled from the base of the cloud in a long downward slant, the white needle moved rapidly toward the red line Grant had carefully striped on the airspeed indicator. *Easy,* he warned himself. *Let's save the wings for another day!*

Out of the corner of his eye, he could enjoy the satisfying bow of the BG's sturdy tapered panels, flexed hard white against the incredible blue of the sky at twelve thousand feet. In clear air again, he eased off the forward pressure and came back on the stick. With a touch of rudder to coordinate things, the vaulting white bird began a glorious wingover that carried it almost as high as it had been a moment ago. Then the nose dropped gracefully down through the horizon. Grant centered his controls and aimed straight at the pile of rock called Keystone Peak, some twenty miles to the east.

Slowly he realized he had been smiling for the last several minutes; an exultant, rewarded smile. It had been worth it all: the saving of money for the sailplane kit, the hours of work through cold winter months and hot, humid summer months. Six hundred hours the brochure that hooked him had promised. It had taken Grant more than twice that long to build the plane and, as his buddies had needled him, he could probably sell it and realize a tidy fifty cents an hour for his blood and sweat and tears.

But it had been worth it—just for the past hour and forty minutes alone. That was how long it had been since he had been released from the towrope of the red-and-white Cessna that had taken him to fifteen hundred feet above the tiny airport called Stone Field.

"Eight-Hotel, this is Stone Field. Come in, Eight-Hotel." The radio speaker's voice crackled in the cockpit and brought Grant out of his dreaming. Squeezing the mike button at the top of the control stick, he leaned his face closer to the microphone clipped to his shirt collar and answered the familiar voice.

"Eight-Hotel," he said, trying to sound casual but knowing the excitement couldn't stay out of his voice. "I'm at eleven-five, Mom, near Tucson. What a ship, and what a day! The thermals are running close to a thousand feet a minute, and the cloud base is better than twelve."

"Wonderful!" replied Florence Stone's steady voice. "No bugs?"

"Aw, come on," Grant said with a mock injured tone. "We build them right, Mom. No sweat. I think I can trim up the rudder linkage a little, and the canopy needs better seals. But she goes like a rocket."

"Fine," his mother said, and she was excited too. "Watch the red line, though. How long will you stay up?"

"Who knows?" Grant said, laughing. "Who cares? Maybe forever."

"They tell me the lift quits when the sun goes down, Grant," his mother said. "Don't forget to make it back to the field. I have to fly over to Tucson for those parts, but I should be home for supper. Okay?"

"Great," Grant said. "Listen, I'll treat tonight. How about Mexican food at Manuel's?"

"You've got yourself a date," she said. "Stone Unicom out."

Grant clicked his mike button twice in acknowledgment and settled back against the cushion of his parachute. Life was great! Life was fantastic! This BG was nothing like the trainers he had checked out in and been flying at Ryan Field with the Soaring Club. Twenty-to-one was their glide angle, and they penetrated a head wind like inflated paper bags. But the BG had a 34-to-1 glide on paper, and was surely better than 30 in real flight. Cruising now at 65 knots between thermals, his sink rate was only a little more than 200 feet a minute.

He was almost to Keystone Peak when he hit the next booming thermal. Grant felt the lift before the vario squealed. The needle of the sensitive rate-of-climb instrument whipped to 500 feet a minute and then higher as he racked the sailplane around to center it better in the upward-rushing column of air. Automatically he kept the yaw string lined up. The eight-inch length of bright-red yarn taped to the canopy in front of him told him when he had his turn coordinated. If it fluttered to the inside during a turn, he was skidding; the outside meant a slip.

His grin broadened, and the magic feeling came back. Power pilots just didn't know. Even his mother didn't know. Sure, a fan up front was nice, and it could keep a pilot from sweating on the way from Point A to Point B. But a power pilot couldn't know the sheer joy of soaring, of standing this great white bird on a wing and lofting it vertically at a thousand feet a minute or better while the ground dropped farther and farther below, of feeling every shift and movement of air, of sensing direction and balance as a bird must sense them.

His first instruction ride in the 2-33 trainer had jolted Grant. They had hit a thermal, and the pilot in the rear seat had banked to what seemed a vertical position. Grant had almost scrambled out of the cockpit trying to stay right side up. Now he could laugh aloud at his ignorance of a year ago. As his new sailplane rose beautifully in tight, circling flight, he looked down the sleek white wing. The sight of it flexing in the slightly bumpy air was a tonic that sent a shiver down his back and along both arms until he could see the goose bumps.

In no time he was at a cloud base again, and he had to use all his willpower to level the wings and dive to get back into the blue air. The FAA ruling was for sailplanes to remain five hundred feet below clouds. Not all pilots observed that rule, and Grant had no desire to meet someone else face to face in the thick mist of a fat cumulus.

To the northeast, the city of Tucson sprawled over gray-white desert and lapped into the foothills of Mount Lemmon. Tucson International's runways formed an elongated ten-thousand-foot cross before him. Davis-Monthan Air Force Base lay five miles farther on, a vast complex of runways, hangars, and parked aircraft. Grant caught sight of

11

jet trails from a pair of fighters boring up from the deck. *The only thing that can climb faster than I can!* he thought. He grinned, keeping an eye on them just in case.

A lot of glider pilots Grant knew made it a practice to fly over Davis-Monthan, but he preferred to skirt the area. His BG was nearly fifty feet in span and bigger than the fighters, but because of its wood-and-fabric construction it would not show well on radar scopes.

Still at nearly twelve thousand feet, Grant decided that the dream of turning his test flight into a cross-country triangle might as well come true. Stone Field to Freeway Airport to Nogales International and home—close to 150 miles. His mother wouldn't believe him when he landed; neither would his buddies in the Soaring Club. But that was okay. They'd believe it when he made his Gold Badge distance flight in a week or two.

Two sailplanes were circling lazily over Ryan Field, but they were far below and didn't answer his radio call. Minutes later he made the turn over Freeway Airport, a single runway in the midst of an industrial park. It got its name from Interstate 10, which angled northwest to Phoenix. Boring south between thermals at ten thousand feet, Grant thought he saw his mother's Cessna far below as she entered the pattern at Tucson International, where she would check the air-freight terminal for engine parts they had ordered for an ailing Twin Comanche. He wanted to call her on the radio, but knew she would be busy with the airport tower.

His watch showed almost three o'clock as he passed to the right of Tucson International. It was another forty miles to Nogales, with little beneath him but rocks and desert, studded with cactus and brush, and cut by washes. There was a dirt strip at Tubac about 2500 feet long, in case he needed it, but he didn't. Working just three thermals, he stayed above eight thousand feet all the way and covered the distance to Nogales in just under an hour. Pretty heady stuff for a guy who had averaged only 23 miles an hour on his Silver C flight of thirty miles! And this was still just a test hop.

The longest—and roughest—leg of his trip was the last one, from Nogales to Stone Field, sixty miles of the meanest-looking terrain he had flown over in the state. Instead of tackling it in a straight line, Grant doubled back almost to Tubac, just in case. The best part of the day was gone, and the lift, when he found it, came to less than 300 feet a minute. Still no sweat, but no need to take chances either.

With forty miles to go he had struggled up in the weakening lift to nearly 10,000 feet above sea level. Stone Field's elevation was 2500 feet, so Grant was about 7500 feet above the ground. With a glide angle of 30, the BG should be able to cover more than forty miles, and surely there would be some lift along the way. There was also a chance of ridge soaring along the Baboquivari Mountains, which rose to seven thousand feet out there ahead of him.

Life is a learning process, somebody had told him, and Grant acquired his new knowledge for the day that afternoon. He left Tubac fat and happy, heading west for a celebration dinner of beef enchiladas and chiles rellenos. Fat, happy, and *dumb,* he realized halfway to the Baboquivari chain.

When flying into a wind of 20 knots, you don't cover thirty-five miles for each mile of altitude. And to reach ridge lift, you have to get on the windward side of a mountain.

With the Baboquivari range already far higher on the horizon than it should have been, Grant suddenly noticed that his variometer had gone berserk. From the moderate sink rate of about 250 feet a minute, which was normal for the speed he was traveling, it suddenly shot to 700 down, then 800. There was a new tension in him now as he felt his body tighten and draw in.

Think up! he told himself. *Where there's sink, there's gotta be lift, man.* But there was none. Desperately he abandoned his straight-line course for home and began to zigzag in the hope of finding rising air—or at least some that wasn't sinking so fast.

From a comfortable altitude of eight thousand feet above sea level, the BG had plummeted to below five thousand when at last he escaped from the sinkhole. That meant he was actually less than three thousand feet above the rough terrain. There was a wide pass through the mountains, and Grant changed course for it quickly, hoping that he could avoid the downdraft on the lee side of the range. He caught himself clearing his throat and realized how nervous he was. *Hang in there,* he cautioned himself. You've got to take the sink with the lift to be a soaring pilot.

Funny how fast a situation could change. A few minutes ago he had had it made. He should have reached home standing on his head. But now, if something didn't happen fast, he would be landing out. Worst of all, he couldn't see anyplace down there in that mess that looked landable.

The thought came that he should call his mother and let her know he might not make it back. But she wouldn't be home from Tucson yet, and there was little point in her flying the Cessna to where he was. Besides, Grant clung to the idea that he was going to get out of this spot anyway. He had been low before in the trainers and in a 1-26—as low as five hundred feet off the deck—and had still got a save in the form of a thermal or a wind slanting up a ridge. If he could just get through the pass and then slide around to the left and work the windward side of the mountain, he

14

should be able to ride the wind high enough to get home.

There were no bad downdrafts as he sneaked through the pass, but the wind must have speeded up as it funneled through the gap in the mountains. To Grant it seemed as if the BG were standing still as far as forward motion was concerned, while the altimeter unwound precious tens of feet from his reserve. He could see saguaro cactus distinctly now, and could almost count the stickers on them. It was going to be tight, and the fear came to him that he might bend his beautiful new bird on its maiden flight. The thought hurt, and he tried to will the craft to stay aloft, to gain a few precious feet and clear the slope sliding by on his left.

Miraculously, Grant was through the pass at last. He banked left, scarcely a hundred feet from the rocks and brush, and felt the delicious upward shudder of the BG as it caught the turbulent rush of wind climbing the range. For the first time in what seemed like an hour, the variometer shrilled happy proof that the sailplane was climbing again. The altimeter stopped winding down, and when Grant leaned forward to tap the glass on the dial, the needle jumped fifty feet up. He could see his vertical progress along the slope, and he could feel it—in the seat of his pants as the sailplane rocked and jumped in eddies of air, in his legs and arms, even in his tense face muscles. This was the name of the game—climbing. Going up instead of down. Slowly his face relaxed, easing the aching muscles in his neck and jaw. The ridge had saved him. He would make it home yet.

Thirty minutes later, however, as the red disk of sun just kissed the inky purple horizon far to the west, Grant faced the fact that the ridge hadn't really saved him at all. Instead, it had trapped him! He could climb five hundred feet above the rocks at the highest point he could find

15

along the mountain, but every time he left the ridge, with his precious hoard of altitude, he could tell in a few miles that it would never last to Stone Field.

In the long, hard shadows, the terrain below him looked more hostile than ever. Even on a stretch of road it would be nearly impossible to set the BG down without hooking a wing on a shoulder, or running into a wash while still rolling at 50 miles an hour. He didn't want to dent his labor of love that way.

If it hadn't been for the wind, he might have made it, but the evening breeze showed no sign of weakening in time to help him. It dragged at the wings and pulled the BG down at an angle so steep it could only lead to a rough landing in the boondocks.

Grant had landed out before. On the first try for his Silver Distance he had been shot down when marine air from the Gulf of California invaded the area and turned the thermals into a soggy, sinking mass. But then there had been a lovely field below him, ground as smooth and level as a tabletop, surveyed and bulldozed for irrigation. Not like the raw desert that waited for him this time.

Okay, chum, he told himself, *you've got maybe another half hour of good light. What are you going to do about it?*

It was a hard question, and he couldn't think of an answer. Earlier, when he first realized the strength of the wind, he had thought of making a quick 180-degree turn and heading downwind for the field at Tubac. But then he had still been fairly high and hadn't hit the discouraging heavy sink. Now it was too late.

In desperation he worked south along the ridge, hanging on to as much altitude as he could, eagerly scanning the terrain ahead for some sign of level field or an unbroken stretch of road long enough to ease the BG onto—say, about seven or eight hundred feet, into the wind. He might

16

as well have wished for ten thousand feet of concrete runway!

The ridge began to drop away below him, and the altimeter matched its descent. Again Grant cleared his throat and suddenly realized he was sweating in spite of the low angle of the sun. Earlier in the day, at the heady twelve-thousand-foot cloud base, he had shivered pleasantly. Now his palms were wet and so was his back, and not all of it was caused by the air temperature. He was in the roughest spot of his short soaring career, and all because he had let himself get cocky. If things didn't improve pretty quickly, he might pay a high price for his carelessness.

He had lost so much altitude that he was about to turn north again when he saw the strip. In fact, he had already begun the right-hand turn when the long white gash loomed ahead and to his left on the desert. At first he thought it was just a straight section of road; he knew of no airstrip in this area. But this was no road. It was a bladed strip, showing faintly against the rough terrain.

Grant's glad shout came of its own accord. Breath whistled through his nostrils as through a relief valve as he lined up his flight path to parallel the strip that loomed a welcome in the dusk. The elevation was about the same as at Stone Field, and checking that against his altimeter, he found that he was fifteen hundred feet above the ground. At maximum glide he should make it, and he forced himself to hold the BG at 45 knots an hour.

He had time now to get on the radio and call home. If necessary he could sack out alongside the sailplane for the night, and his mother could come and tow him home in the morning. No sweat, after all.

But there was no answer to his repeated calls, and at five hundred feet he gave up and concentrated on the landing. He was used to spoilers on the club gliders, but the

BG had flaps. As it turned out, he didn't use them. Still at maximum glide, he slid quietly over the cactus and brush at the east end of the strip and, seconds later, flared carefully for his first landing in his own sailplane. He greased it on, hardly knowing when he touched.

A relieved grin creased Grant's sweaty face as he held the craft balanced on its one wheel and let it roll as far as it would toward the shack at the end of the strip. There might be a phone there, and he could call his mother.

He kept the wings level until the BG sighed to a full stop, still several hundred feet from the shack. Then the right tip dropped slowly until it touched the ground with a hollow bang and a puff of dust. Grant released the canopy. Although the sun was down and the field in dark shadow, it was still hot as an oven, and he was eager to get out and shed the parachute.

Gently he eased the canopy to the ground and unhooked his harness. He was surprised that he was so stiff until he remembered that this had been his longest flight yet in a sailplane. Wearily he climbed out of the cockpit, shut off the switches, and unhooked the battery. He was so busy he didn't hear anyone approaching until the voice rasped just behind him.

"All right, fella, turn around. Slow."

Still stooping over the canopy, Grant whirled in surprise —and found himself looking down the barrel of a gun in the hand of a bearded man! Just behind that man was another, also heavily bearded. Both men wore faded jeans and dirty T-shirts. The one with the gun was flabby, with a belly hanging over his belt. The other man was about Grant's build. He guessed they were in their middle thirties, although the beards made it hard to tell. It was a strange welcoming committee, and he blinked his eyes, wondering if he was imagining the whole thing.

18

CHAPTER 2

It was the first time Grant had ever been threatened with a gun, but there was such an odd, unreal tone to the whole thing that he had no feeling of fear. Instead, shocked and angry, he heard himself say in a tight voice, *"Don't* point that at me!"

"It's a kid," the second man said, and Grant thought he sounded relieved.

"Turn around, kid," said the man with the gun, his face as expressionless as that of a bull. "Lean over the wing. Frisk him."

Grant started to refuse and almost reached out to push the gun barrel away. The man was shorter than he, and the whole situation seemed ridiculous—like something that fit better into a poor TV movie. But the hard look in the man's eyes changed his mind, and he realized suddenly that the gun was no joke. They meant business. Slowly Grant turned and braced himself against the wing while the other man satisfied himself that he was unarmed.

"Okay, kid," the fat man said. "Turn around. What are you doing here?"

"I'm not selling Fuller brushes," Grant said tightly. "What does it look like I'm doing?"

"Don't get smart, kid. You can't afford it," the second man said. "You could be in big trouble for trespassing."

"Check the cockpit," said the man with the gun, and for a second Grant thought he was being spoken to. Then the other man bent over the BG's cockpit and began hauling out the parachute.

"Hey, cut it out!" Grant protested, picking up the backpack from the ground and setting it on the wing. "Are you crazy?"

"Anybody's crazy, it's somebody who don't know a gun can go off," said the fat man. "Kid, you shut up and get over there and sit down." He pointed some distance away, and reluctantly Grant moved off and squatted down. The other man poked around the back of the seat, then suddenly cursed and flung up one hand.

"How do you get this stupid backrest out?" he demanded, holding his gashed hand.

"It helps to know what you're doing," Grant told him, not moving, and trying to keep from smiling his satisfaction. There were some sharp aluminum angles he hadn't yet rounded with a file, and the man must have snagged himself on one of them.

"All right, kid," the fat man said, waving the gun threateningly. "Get that panel out of there, and do it fast. Let's see what you've got in this crate."

"I can tell you and save us all a lot of trouble," Grant said. "There's space back there for an oxygen tank, plus storage for tie-downs, bedroll, and stuff like that. Right now it's empty because I just finished the sailplane a few days ago."

"I'm from Missouri," the man said, still waving the gun. "Get that panel off and show me."

Grant did as he was told, and then both men in turn stuck their heads into the space behind the seat. Finally

20

they seemed satisfied, and the man with the gun shoved his weapon into his pocket.

"You mind if I put the panel back?" Grant asked. "I want to get the canopy on before somebody steps on it."

"No hurry, kid," the other man said. "It'll wait. Let's go over to the shack and have a talk."

"I'm in a hurry to call home and get my sailplane out of here," Grant protested. "I've had a pretty rough day."

"It might get rougher in a minute. Come on. We're going to talk."

The three of them walked single file, with Grant in the middle, through the sand to the rough board shack at the end of the strip. It was dark inside, and the thin man lit a kerosine lamp on the table in a corner of the room. There were two chairs, and Grant sat in one at the command of his captors. The man with the gun sat in the other one, and his partner went outside.

"Take it from the top," said the man facing him. In the lamplight he looked meaner than ever with his full beard. "Who put you up to landing here?"

"Nobody put me up to anything," Grant said wearily. "I was trying to make it back to my airport and got shot down. I spotted your strip and landed. That's all."

"This isn't an airstrip," the man said tightly. "Understand?"

"It'll do till one comes along," Grant said, smiling in spite of himself. "Look, what's all this cloak-and-dagger stuff anyway?"

"I'm asking the questions," the man said, obviously irritated at Grant's attempt at humor. "You're trespassing, kid. You could be in big trouble."

"I'd be in bigger trouble if I'd cracked up out there," Grant said angrily. "How did I know there were two nuts down here?"

A blast of profanity silenced him, and a hand shot across the table and grabbed him by the shoulder. "You're too lippy, kid," the man said, his eyes snapping. "Suppose I get the cops and prefer charges?"

"Great," Grant said. "Just so I can get my sailplane out of this crazy place." He was cut off as the door opened and the other man burst in.

"Joe's coming," he said to the man with the gun. "At least I hope that's who it is. If this kid's glider attracted someone else, we may have to—"

"Knock it off," the fat man said, getting to his feet. "Keep an eye on him while I go see who it is. Watch him good. He thinks he's pretty tough."

Hoping it was a deputy sheriff or some other law-enforcement officer, Grant sat glaring across the table at his captor. The man grinned at him and pulled out a switchblade knife, which he snapped open and flipped into the tabletop, where it quivered back and forth for a while.

Outside there was the sound of an approaching vehicle. Then a car door slammed, and a moment later footsteps thudded toward the shack. The man with the gun and a third man entered. The newcomer didn't match the other two. He was well dressed and clean-shaven, and he smiled apologetically as he came in.

"That's a beautiful bird out there," he said. "Looks like you ran out of lift, eh?"

"Right," Grant admitted, trying to comprehend the sudden turn of the tide. "I was beginning to think I'd run out of luck too. These guys seem to suspect I'm a spy or something."

"Forgive my colleagues," the newcomer said, laughing. "It's just that we . . . uh, have to be very careful in our work. Right, boys?"

The others grunted but said nothing.

22

"My name is Reese," the third man said. "Joe Reese. Yours?"

"Grant Stone," Grant said, getting up and pushing his chair out of the way.

For a second or two the man seemed startled. A row of wrinkles creased his forehead, but they vanished before he spoke again. "My pleasure, Grant," he said, reaching over to shake hands. "Look, we're in a bind, so let's figure a way to get you out of here. Okay?"

"I've been trying to do that ever since I landed," Grant said. "Could I at least call my mother and let her know I'm all right?"

"We'll do better than that," Reese said. "I'll have you back at Stone Field in an hour, so you can pick up your trailer and come back for your bird. How's that?"

"Great," Grant said, smiling for the first time since he had landed the BG. "Too bad you weren't here when I landed. But how do I know these guys won't mess up my sailplane while we're gone?"

"They won't," Reese promised.

"Look . . . Reese," the man with the gun said. "Are you sure—"

"I'm positive," Reese said. "Come on, let's get on the road."

A minute later Grant was latching the BG's canopy securely and tying on its cloth cover so that if the wind picked up, the sand wouldn't etch the Plexiglas. Reese helped him, shining a flashlight in the growing darkness.

"You built her yourself?" the man asked, with an interest that surprised Grant.

"Right," he said. "From a kit, though. My mother helped with sewing the fabric and a lot of other stuff."

"Great," Reese said. "I've always wanted to fly a sailplane. Someday, maybe. . . . Hey, we better go."

Reese drove the Ford as though he knew the rutted gravel road like the back of his hand. And he handled it like a dirt-track race driver, cornering at speeds Grant couldn't believe. After one hairy slide on a sharp turn, he almost protested, but the man behind the wheel seemed so confident that he bit down on the words and held tighter to the door handle, grateful for the seat belt. After all, he was in a hurry to let his mother know he was okay.

Reese talked briefly about the two men back at the strip, apologizing for their lack of tact. But he said they had good reason. "They're okay," he said, smiling at Grant. "Just doing their job."

"What job is that?" Grant asked. "This is the first time I ever had a gun poked in my face."

"Well, you just happened to stumble onto something complicated," Reese told him, and Grant noticed that the smile was gone. "I wish you hadn't, because that makes it sticky for all of us. I can't tell you much more. You'll just have to trust me. Okay?"

"I don't know," Grant said, puzzled. "I appreciate the way you put them down, though, and this ride sure helps. Hey, we're almost to the airport."

"Right," Reese said. To Grant's surprise, he switched off the headlights and then the ignition as well, so that they coasted silently to a stop near the hangar. "I'll just drop you here," Reese said apologetically. "I have business in Phoenix tonight. But my two friends will help you get your sailplane on the trailer. It must be off our strip before daylight. Okay?"

"Why?" Grant demanded. "Look, there's something funny . . ."

With a quick movement that startled Grant into thinking the man was reaching for a gun, Reese dropped a hand to his back pocket and whipped out a billfold. Quickly he

24

flipped it toward Grant. In it was an official-looking card with a small color photograph of Reese on it. That was about all Grant had a chance to see.

"You'll have to trust me," the big man said. "Forget what happened tonight. Have a great time with your new bird. Maybe our paths will cross again." He reached out a hand, they shook, and then the black car was gone.

Grant was still standing there by the road when he heard his mother call. Slowly he turned and headed for the house, shaking his head in confusion.

"It's me, Mom," he yelled. "I'm fine. Sorry I couldn't let you know sooner but . . . I had some problems."

She was shaken—he could tell that by the way she hugged him before they went inside. The excitement and pleasure of the test hop were forgotten as he told her quickly all that had happened since he touched down at the strip forty miles to the south.

"Oh, my," his mother said in a frightened voice when he had finished. "Grant, I don't like this at all. We'd better call the sheriff."

"No," Grant said slowly. "What we better do first is go get the BG and bring it home." He was worried too, but a big part of his concern was for the white bird that meant so much to him. Suppose he *was* trespassing on private property? Maybe his sailplane could be confiscated. The two bearded men struck him as the kind who would do anything. And there was the puzzle about Reese, the tall, lean man who seemed so different from his two friends. There was vague confusion in Grant's mind about the man, an odd feeling he couldn't understand.

"All right, Grant, if you're sure," his mother agreed uncertainly. "But you'd better take Harry along for safety. Oh, wait. You must be starved."

"I'm fine," Grant said, moving toward the door. "We

25

can be back in a couple of hours, and I'll grab a bite then. You call Harry while I hook up the trailer."

In fifteen minutes they pulled out from the airport, the long sailplane trailer tracking smoothly behind the pickup, its running lights glowing in the darkness. The truck cab was hot inside, and when they hit the dirt road, it was a toss-up which was worse—rolling up the windows or eating dust.

After Harry had been briefed on the situation, Grant had little to say. The thrill and excitement that he had hoped to share with both Harry and his mother had been effectively squelched, and Grant drove silently along the road south, far slower than the stranger had brought him home.

He had watched the odometer of the Ford on the trip up, so he was able to gauge when they had reached the mysterious strip. Even then he almost missed the faint twin ruts branching from the road to the west. There was no moon, and they had almost reached the shack before he saw it and the pale white shape of the BG beyond. He tapped the horn button lightly, so the two gorillas couldn't accuse him of trying to sneak up on them, then braked to a stop.

The door swung open, and the two men came out, one carrying a flashlight.

"I came back for my sailplane," Grant said.

"You need help?" a gruff voice demanded.

"No, thanks," he told them. "We'll make out all right."

There was a muffled curse, and the bearded men went back inside. Grant drove slowly to where the BG waited, and with Harry signaling by flashlight, he backed the trailer until its rear door was about six feet from the nose of the sailplane.

De-rigging was awkward in the dark, but they managed. First he and Harry rolled the craft forward until the nose was secure in the wheeled cradle in the trailer. Then they detached the wings and slid them into the racks on each side of the trailer. The big mechanic insisted on carrying the heavy ends of the wings, and that was fine with Grant. He removed the stabilizer and had it ready for stowing by the time Harry had the fuselage inside. Grant carefully closed the rear door of the trailer and locked it. As he did, he felt a load being lifted from him, and for the first time in several hours, the tightness left his muscles.

"Let's go," he said, and they climbed back into the cab.

It was nearly midnight when they finally pulled into town. Manuel's neon sign still winked on the left side of the road, and Grant suddenly was aware that his backbone was about to meet his belt buckle.

"How about some supper?" he said. "And I'll tell you all about my flight. I'll call Mom and she can join us."

"I'll settle for pie and coffee," Harry said. "But I am curious to know why you didn't make it back to the field." He grinned as they climbed down from the truck, and Grant remembered all the kidding he had taken from the beefy mechanic while he was building the sailplane. Harry didn't believe in powerless flight.

By the time he had finished his supper and described his flight in detail for them, Grant had almost forgotten the unpleasantness that had ended it. His mother was smiling, sharing his enthusiasm for the clean white craft they had worked on together.

"When are you going to let me check you out in sail-planes, Mom?" he demanded. "It's time you had some fun too."

"I'm afraid I'm too accustomed to propellers, dear,"

she told him. "Habit dies hard. Besides, aren't you going to be spending all your spare time this summer winning contests and completing badge flights?"

"That's for sure," Grant said, draining the last of his coffee and picking up the check. "I learned enough today to make Gold Distance on my next flight."

"Good luck," Harry said. "Look, thanks for the pie, but could I go home? We've got that engine to check out tomorrow, and I need my beauty sleep."

Once the BG was safely in the hangar, Grant showered and climbed into bed. Tired as he was, he had to think the day out and try to make some sense out of it. As he looked back, the incident at the tiny strip seemed more unreal than ever, more like hokey TV melodrama.

Maybe the best thing to do was take Joe Reese's advice to forget about it and concentrate on the sheer joy of flying the sailplane. He had his BG back, unharmed. He had completed his first flight, made a good landing in the boondocks, and he could put a trip of well over a hundred miles in his logbook in the morning.

Well, you won some and you lost some, so what if he had had a slight problem with two ding-a-lings out in the desert?

Still, it wasn't that easy to put out of his mind. Something bothered him about the whole crazy setup, and he woke in the middle of the night with a sudden awareness of what it was that bugged him the most—that third man, Reese.

Grant went over everything that had happened very carefully, every action and every word anybody had said. When he finished, he was sure his memory was accurate. When Reese offered to bring him back home, he had immediately mentioned Stone Field. And that was funny, because how did he know where Grant lived? Besides that,

28

why had learning Grant's name seemed to shake the guy for a moment?

Grant knew this wasn't one of those things that would go away if he just ignored it. It was a long time before he got to sleep again.

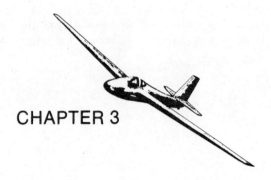

CHAPTER 3

Grant was dreaming about flying the BG, a fantastic flight to altitudes of bitter cold where he was about to black out for lack of oxygen, when the racket of the twin Comanche's new engine jarred him awake. Still groggy, he rolled out of bed and reached for his alarm clock on the dresser. It was already eight thirty. He had forgotten to set the alarm in all the excitement of the night before. Angry with himself, he went into the bathroom. This was the first weekday he could remember when he hadn't been up and at work by seven thirty.

The house was empty. Grant gulped down a bowlful of cereal and then ate a peach as he walked over to the hangar. The gold-and-white Comanche gleamed like new on the apron in front of the open hangar. Harry had finally shut down the Lycoming engine, apparently satisfied with his overhaul. The big mechanic waved a greeting from the wing as he cleaned the windshield.

Grant returned the wave and shook his head in embarrassment. They shouldn't have let him sleep in, with all the work that had to be done today. He had played hookey from chores to check out the BG. Now he had to make up for that.

Not yet nine o'clock, and it was already hot. The sky was blue overhead, but the mountains in the distance rippled in haze. Grant noted that there were no cumulus clouds yet. Dry as it was, none might materialize during the day. But there would be thermals.

A Cessna 150 buzzed high to the north, and the radio speaker crackled as Grant walked toward the little office to find his mother. "Stone Unicom, this is Cessna Five-One-Nine-Nine-Tango. What is your active runway, please?"

"Nine-Nine-Tango, this is Stone Unicom," his mother's voice answered, slightly metallic by virtue of electronics and the loudspeaker. "Active runway, Two-Seven. The wind is calm."

Grant knew the red-and-white plane. In a few moments it would be shooting raggedy touch-and-go landings on their blacktopped runway. Later on, a pair of Grumman Ag-Cats from Central Dusting would be screaming in at regular intervals for gas as they sprayed cotton acreage to the north.

At eleven o'clock Grant had a student who was about ready to solo, but was too self-conscious about it. Pushing new pilots out of the nest was a serious business, and Grant knew he had a decision to make about that solo soon. But he did not have to decide for two hours yet. In the meantime he had a lot of other things to do.

"Good morning," his mother called from her desk as he entered the office. She was working on the books, getting reports ready for their accountant so Grant could take them along when he drove the pickup to town.

"You did a bad thing," he told her, shaking his head in disapproval. "Why didn't you wake me up?"

"I didn't have the heart to," she answered, smiling. "You had a rough day yesterday. Did you get some breakfast?"

31

"Right. It's a good thing Harry fired up the Comanche or I'd have slept till noon."

"Don't bet on it," his mother teased. "I'll have these records ready for Mr. Jones in five minutes. You can load those oil drums on the pickup. And don't forget we need some weed killer for along the south taxiway."

"I wish I *could* forget," Grant said soulfully. "I'm the guy who's going to have to spray the stuff."

"We lead a busy life," his mother said. "But it keeps us out of mischief."

The radio blared again as Nine-Nine-Tango told the world in general he was going to shoot some touch-and-go landings. Grant watched the sunburst-striped Cessna slant down for a landing of sorts as he walked toward the dusty pickup. They led a busy life here for sure, he agreed, but his mother always worked harder than he, or even than Harry. It had been like that for as long as he could remember. It must be hard for a woman alone to make a living for herself and her son.

With a twinge of conscience, Grant climbed into the truck and hit the starter. The ancient engine wheezed and finally caught, but he knew it wouldn't last much longer. The money they had spent for the sailplane kit had been earmarked for a replacement truck, but his mother had insisted on getting the sailplane. It had been an advance present for his eighteenth birthday and graduation, all rolled into one big 50-foot package. His mother was quite a gal.

Grant had only the faintest recollection of his father. A long time ago his mother had done her best to explain to him how she and Mike Stone had agreed to call it quits. The handsome ex–Air Force fighter pilot had taken the Cadillac, plus all the money they had in the bank, and headed

32

for parts unknown. Florence Stone had been left with the pickup truck—the same one Grant was driving now—and the airport that Mike had bought after he left the service.

The whole thing was hazy in Grant's mind. His mother had been charitable about her ex-husband, but there must have been good reason for the breakup. Grant thought it involved a drinking problem and some dealings in stolen aircraft which had been more than she could put up with. His mother had been a teacher before her marriage in a posh eastern school for girls. Arizona must have seemed like the last frontier to the slim Connecticut bride, but she stuck it out, even after the breakup of the six-year-old marriage. Pride maybe, plus a young son to take care of.

Mike had left Flo with a mortgaged, weed-infested museum of aging aircraft twelve years ago. It wasn't flying itself that had kept her on the tiny strip, which had been an auxiliary field back in World War II, although Mike Stone had taught her to fly tolerably well. Flo contributed business sense to the operation, an aptitude most likely inherited from her father, who was a successful factory manager in New England. Today the small airport was prospering. Flo had two mechanics, three instructors, including herself and Grant, and a healthy annual gross—a fact that continued to amaze Irv Jones, the gray-haired accountant who had long ago advised Grant's mother to sell out or even "give the dump back to the county." Still, cash was always short in the Stone household.

Grant could remember sleeping in a partitioned corner of the old hangar, listening to galvanized iron sheets flapping when strong winds blew out of the southwest. His first chores had included pouring old crankcase oil in the cracks of the runway to kill weeds, and answering the phone while his mother took students up for flight instruction.

33

There was a house now, small but comfortable. The new hangar was a gleaming steel prefab they were still paying on. They had twenty tie-downs outside, most of them rented, plus three aircraft of their own—four, Grant corrected himself with a grin. The BG was as much of an aircraft as the 150, the newer Citabria, or the Cessna 182 they had flown to Connecticut two years ago when they visited his mother's family.

He couldn't really remember when he hadn't been at home in an airplane. He could fly well at age twelve, and he soloed at eight o'clock in the morning on his sixteenth birthday. Since then he had piled up 1142 hours—plus whatever he had added yesterday in the BG. He had his private, commercial, and certified flight instructor tickets, and if it hadn't been for his sudden interest in soaring, he would have been instrument-rated by now.

Last year he had landed the 150 at Ryan Field near Tucson, curious about the sailplanes flying all over the area. A contest had been in progress, and he had learned, to his amazement, that those guys were climbing into craft with no engines, heading out for Prescott, and returning—making the three-hundred-mile round trip. Two weeks later he took his first ride with the Tucson Soaring Club and was hooked. The Brieglieb BG-12/16 was the result, and if all went well, he would enter the next contest.

Grant took care of things in town, filling the oil drums at the refinery and adding two cans of rank-smelling weed killer. The accountant had been out, but Grant left the records on his desk with a note. On the way back he picked up a new tail pipe and muffler for the pickup. He'd have to put them on before the police ticketed him for noise pollution. It was a quarter to eleven when he parked the truck in the shade of the hangar.

34

His mother was pumping gas for a Cessna 182 that flew parachute jumpers. The plane's door had been removed, and the pilot sat on the floor with his feet dangling out. Grant waved and the pilot asked when he was going up for a static-line jump. Grant grinned and shook his head. He had made one jump, about a year ago, just to satisfy himself. It was okay, but he'd rather fly than sky dive.

His student, more nervous-looking than usual, was sitting in the office thumbing through a copy of *Flying* and trying hard to seem nonchalant. He looked up and tried a grin, but the result was pathetic. Today wasn't the day, Grant decided, as he grinned back.

"Hi, Roger. Looks like a good day for coordination exercises. Okay?"

"Okay!" Roger said, leaping happily to his feet. "I was wondering when we could get back to that. Let's go!" He looked like a condemned man just given a reprieve as he ground out his cigarette in the big ashtray and raced for the door.

Roger did fairly well with his flying in spite of turbulent air. Maybe by his next lesson he'd be ready to climb into the 150 alone.

During lunch Grant finally got a chance to take a breather.

"How's your star student?" Harry asked, as they sat at the counter eating sandwiches from the machine and drinking cold pop.

"This is the critical time," Grant admitted. "But he'll make it. He's really better than he thinks he is, and I've got to prove that to him without scaring him off."

"Any message from Mr. Jones?" his mother asked.

"Nope. He wasn't there. We're doing okay, aren't we? Money-wise, I mean."

"Money-wise we are doing okay," his mother assured

him. "Especially if Harry is through playing with Dr. Christopherson's Comanche."

"Harry is through," the mechanic said, nodding. "That engine is good for another two thousand hours. I hate to see that beautiful ship go, though. It kind of gives us class, you know."

"Maybe we can buy it from the doctor," Grant joked. "You want me to ask him when I deliver it this afternoon?"

"If you have seventy-five thousand dollars, go ahead," his mother said, laughing. "Handle that plane with care, Grant. You know how fussy the Christophersons are about it."

"Roger-Dodger, Mom. I promise not to do any snap rolls on the way over. I'll get all my kicks in the BG."

"Good," she said. "Starting when?"

"At the contest Sunday," he said. "If that's okay with you guys."

"You'll miss church?" she asked in disappointment.

"I should be able to make the early service. The contest won't get started till about noon."

"Don't run out of wind," Harry warned. "But speaking of the Comanche, how are you going to get home after you deliver it?"

"The worst possible way." Grant groaned. "I'll catch a bus, I guess."

"Beats walking. Come on," Harry taunted. "I'll teach you how to start the engines."

The sleek twin-engined Piper Comanche was a plush aircraft, Grant had to admit. If you couldn't fly sailplanes, it would be a pretty good consolation prize. Someday, when he was rich, he'd like to have one. The 160-horsepower engines ran as smoothly as whipped cream, but he resisted the temptation to pull up steeply on takeoff. Instead he forced himself to fly a sedate pattern: a ninety-degree turn to the left at four hundred feet and then a neat forty-five to leave the pattern.

He adjusted prop pitch, leaned the throttles, and settled back in the comfortable seat as the plane bored its way east. Far ahead of him, over Mount Lemmon and to the south, there were cumulus clouds. Somewhere, somebody was having a ball in a sailplane, and the thought brought yesterday's flight back to his mind sharply. Almost without realizing it, he banked the Comanche to the right, until his heading paralleled the road cutting through the desert toward Mexico. He would fly over the mysterious little strip he had found. Maybe it wouldn't even be there, and he could forget the whole crazy business. Maybe the two weird characters with the beards would have rolled it up by now and hauled it off for some other monkey business somewhere else. Which would be great good riddance.

At 190 miles an hour, it didn't take long to reach the strip. Scanning the terrain a mile below him, Grant was amazed at how hard it was to spot. The low angle of the sun must have helped make it so clearly visible yesterday. By accident or planning, it was a beautiful job of camouflage. Only the small shack at the west end made him sure he was looking at the strip and not just at an abandoned stretch of road. There was no sign of life at all.

And then, without consciously deciding to do so, Grant suddenly knew he was going to land and do some investigating. He had promised his mother he would handle the newly overhauled airplane with tender loving care, and he knew he should have sense enough to leave well enough alone. But what had happened yesterday had really bugged him, and he was still angry that the men could get by with that stuff. Ten to one, there was some funny business going on, in spite of the smooth performance by the third man of the trio.

Checking for smoke or dust to give him the wind direction, Grant cut power and circled over the strip. A weed fire to the north reassured him that the wind was still out of the west, where it ought to be. There was a fair breeze now, probably 10 knots or so on the ground. So much the better for landing the Comanche on the short strip.

Grant dropped half flaps and flew a careful pattern at 85 miles an hour. There was enough drift on his base leg for him to be sure of the wind. He left the flaps where they were, just in case he had to make a go-around, and judged his descent carefully so he could touch down as soon as possible.

The plane kissed the ground softly, and he held it straight for the quick roll-out. He was sweating just a little when he cut the switches and opened the door. It had been a crazy notion, but he was here now. He moved fast to get his detective work over and done with.

Dropping from the wing, he ran the short distance to the shack and yanked at the door. It yielded only an inch or so, and then he saw a padlock close to the top. Impatiently he got both hands on the knob and heaved as hard as he could. The hasp groaned and shivered and finally let go, tumbling Grant backward, so that he had to hang on to keep from falling. He was in it now. Didn't they call this breaking and entering? But something told him the users of the shack were not likely to prefer charges.

Inside, the room looked the same: table, two chairs, and the kerosine lamp, now nearly empty of fuel. A few paperback books lay on a bookcase that sagged against the far wall. And that was it. Confused, Grant rummaged in the ill-fitting drawer in the table, felt along the rafters and over the windows. He wasn't sure what he was looking for, but there ought to be *something*. Those beards weren't just on a cookout there in the boondocks. They could be stealing airplanes, rustling cattle—or running dope. And he would bet on number three.

Grant gave up and went to the door. Maybe they had

completed the part that this place played in their operation. Anyway, he had eased his curiosity, and there seemed to be no more he could do about it. Now he had better get the plane back into the blue before Dr. Christopherson called Grant's mother and asked what had happened to his beautiful toy.

He heard an airplane engine as he came out into bright sunlight, and the sound cut through him like a knife. He knew for a split second how a thief must feel when he is about to be caught—sick at his stomach and weak in the legs. Automatically he started to run for the Comanche, even before he was sure the plane overhead was going to land.

He caught himself and glanced up, hoping it was a casual flight that posed no threat. But he wasn't that lucky. The plane was an old cabin job, painted dark blue or black, and it was coming down like a bomb, racked up in a steep slip that would end halfway down the dirt strip.

For a second Grant considered racing for the Comanche and trying somehow to get it off the ground—around, under, or over the approaching plane. If it had been his own, he probably would have done that, because the memory of the gun and the vicious switchblade was suddenly sharp in his mind. But a downwind takeoff from this vest-pocket strip would be hairy. He might wash out the beautiful twin engine, and his mother's business with it.

There was one thing to do, and he did it. Running to the plane, he climbed in and started the engines. There was a chance he could bluff the other craft off the runway, and somehow get into the air and away.

But it wasn't his day. The plane—it was a Stinson, he saw now—bored straight in, correcting the slip at the last second to touch down hot and on one wheel. It rolled straight for Grant, white smoke blending with dust as the pilot locked the brakes. And when it stopped, there was no place for the Comanche to go. Wishing desperately for a gun, preferably a machine gun, Grant sat tensely in the cabin, watching as two men tumbled out of the other craft. He had the feeling that he knew them from a previous meeting. He was right.

Grant obeyed the fat man's signal to chop the engines promptly, mainly because the man had made another, stronger signal with the gun, aiming it at Grant's head. The twin props jerked to a stop, and there was only the wind hissing along the fuselage and shivering the wings. With a sinking feeling, Grant obeyed the further signal to get out. He raised his hands too, because it seemed like a smart thing to do.

A long blast of foul language told Grant that the men had recognized him. He dropped awkwardly to the ground on stiff legs. The thought came too late that he should have got on the radio with a Mayday call for help, and he wanted to kick himself in disgust. On the heels of that lost hope came the idea that maybe he could fake it, *tell* them he had put in such a call. But his mouth seemed full of cotton, and he didn't try.

"Kid, you have got to be in a rut," the man with the gun said. "Don't tell me you ran out of lift again."

"I told Joe we were crazy to let the kid go," the pilot said hotly. "He's probably a narc!"

"I figured you were running dope," Grant said, the words filtering their way through the cotton.

"You're a real brain," the fat man said sarcastically. "Let's have the whole story."

"Hey, he busted the lock off," the other man yelled from the shack before Grant could respond.

"Looking for evidence?" the fat man asked savagely. He moved in close and shoved the gun into Grant's stomach.

40

It was hard and bruising, and the muzzle felt big enough for a cannonball to come out of it.

Grant remembered stories about cool hands who simply grabbed a gun and held it in such a way that the safety was on. That was a joke, and his hands stayed high.

"You should have left well enough alone, kid," the man said harshly. "If we were through here, I'd kill you right now and bury you out there in the dunes. I'd even get a nice new plane as a bonus. But we need this place for a while yet. You've got one more chance to keep breathing. You want to hear how?"

"Yes," Grant whispered hoarsely, as the gun barrel prodded deeper.

"Okay, listen. You go to the narcs, and I promise you true, there's *two* people going to die. Your mother will be first, kid. And after you've seen it, you get yours. Is that plain enough?"

Grant licked his lips and nodded. The thought of death for himself was terrifying, but danger to his mother was worse.

"Okay. You develop a galloping case of amnesia then. You never heard of this place, understand? You dreamed it all."

Grant nodded again, and the gun moved away. This was no TV hokum. The bearded man meant every word he said. With the gun he motioned toward the open door of the Comanche.

"Get this plane out of here before I decide to keep it anyway," he said. "And remember, if you blab to anybody, you both get it. Her first. Now beat it."

Afterward Grant couldn't remember much about his takeoff. The second man had taxied the black Stinson off the strip, and Grant had rolled the Comanche to the far

41

end, spun it on a braked wheel, and taken off without incident. Then he sat at the controls like a robot, flying automatically—almost in a daze—to Tucson International. He made the landing all right and left the plane in Dr. Christopherson's T-hangar. Fortunately, the owner wasn't there, for it would have been hard for Grant to talk coherently after what had happened at the secret airstrip.

Grant knew the dope scene. He had lost two good friends to the stuff. One was at the State Prison in Florence, the other at the State Hospital in Phoenix. Because of the proximity to a source of supply in Mexico, dope was perhaps a worse problem here than in many other places. Not long ago there had been a scandal that rocked an entire small town north of Tucson. Among the many young people busted as pushers were graduating seniors Grant knew.

Still fighting the shakes, he caught the city bus to downtown Tucson and walked to the Greyhound terminal. He was glad now for the long, slow ride back home, for it gave him time to settle down and stop shaking. It gave him time to think, too.

But even after thinking hard, he still hadn't solved anything when he stepped off the bus across from the airport.

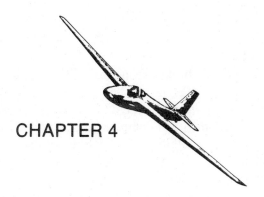

CHAPTER 4

Somehow Grant got through the rest of the day without his mother's learning of his problem. She knew something was bothering him, but he put her off by saying it was an upset stomach and went to bed early. He didn't sleep much. But he did evolve a plan, the only solution he could think of, and he tried to sell his mother on the idea at breakfast.

"A *vacation?*" she repeated in surprise, smiling at him over her newspaper. We've already been to San Diego for a week. Isn't that enough for one summer? Besides, running an airport is fun, fun, fun. You told me that yourself once."

"When I was a nutty little kid," he objected. "Look, Mom, it's been a long time since you saw your folks. Why don't you hop on a jet and go back east for a visit? I can run this ranch for a while. I owe you that . . . after all my goofing off on that BG."

"I think you're trying to get rid of me," she said, putting down the paper to stare at him in surprise. "It was just last week I talked with my parents, Grant. Next year, maybe—"

"Come on," he urged. "We can afford it. There's some money in the bank, and business shouldn't get any worse."

"Yes, and I have a high-school graduate who wants to go to engineering school." She reached over and put her hand on his. "A graduate who is very considerate of his mother, I might add. And she appreciates it. But no more vacations this year, Grant." When she shook her head that way, he knew it was final.

"Mom . . ." Grant broke off in frustration, and her look changed.

"Something's the matter, isn't it?" she asked gently. "I knew it yesterday when you complained of not feeling well. Did they . . . is it something to do with those men you ran into the other day?"

"If you'd just be reasonable, Mom," he begged, "I could handle this mess and get it over with."

"Uh-oh, wild horses won't get me away now," his mother said. "Let's have it—the truth, the whole truth, and nothing but the truth!"

Grant was in so deep there was no use denying it. He admitted the whole stupid bit, apologizing for risking the doctor's plane to check out the deserted field.

"Oh, my," his mother said when he had finished. She got up distractedly and walked to the kitchen window, as though intruders might show up at any minute. "My brave son. You were going to get me safely out of the way and then go to the sheriff."

"Or somebody," Grant said. "Mom, I can take care of myself, but I don't want you to get hurt."

"I'm proud of you," his mother said, turning from the window. "I know you can take care of yourself. But dodging bullets is something else, Grant. We must do something, but I don't know just what. Maybe I should go talk to Mr. Jones."

"Mom, you think Mr. Jones can do everything," Grant said wearily. "He's a good bookkeeper, but dope smuggling is out of his line."

"He could find out in a few days."

"Sure, and in the meantime something happens and those gorillas come after you. Look, I got us into this, and I've got to get us out."

"It's not your fault! It's those terrible men," his mother told him, coming over and putting her arms around him. "You hear about these things, but you never think they can come so close to you. That plane we had stolen five years ago—I always thought it was smugglers who took it."

"So what do we do?" Grant demanded, pulling away. "Those apes are probably junkies themselves. They get it wholesale."

"I'll go back east, if you'll come with me," his mother offered, her eyes brightening. "We could notify the authorities once we were safe."

"Sure, and come back to find the airport wrecked," Grant said.

"Not with Harry here. And we could ask the sheriff to patrol the field."

"Twenty-four hours a day? Mom, I can't leave."

"Neither can I," his mother said resolutely. "So what do we do?"

"I guess there's just one thing we *can* do," Grant said in defeat. "We can keep quiet—as the man warned me."

"Maybe they're not running dope," his mother added. "You aren't positive, are you?"

"Of course not. They may be Eagle Scouts working on an ecology badge, for all I know," he snapped. "Okay, you're right. Maybe it is something else. They could be spies or something. That third guy had an official-looking ID card he flipped at me, the way FBI agents do on TV."

"Do you suppose you could contact *him* again?" his mother asked, sitting down at the table again.

"I don't know," Grant said, staring out the window. "I had the idea once that he was dealing with these guys just

45

to get the goods on them. How's that for a cornball cloak-and-dagger plot?"

"I'm sure such things are done," his mother said. "Sit down and finish your cereal."

"Who can eat? So you think we should make like those three monkeys Grandma has on her mantelpiece. 'See no evil, hear no evil, speak no evil.' And get you a bulletproof vest, just in case."

"I hate not to be a good citizen," his mother said. "But really, what could we tell the sheriff? Maybe that *is* private property down there. Those men could be looking for gold or uranium or something else. The threats might just be to scare you."

"Well, they sure worked," Grant said, laughing shortly. "Mom, I thought for sure I was going to be an orphan."

"It's settled then?" his mother asked eagerly. "We keep diplomatically quiet about the whole thing? At least for the time being?"

"Cowardly is a better word," Grant suggested.

"That's not true, Grant," his mother objected. Then her face brightened and she stood up. "Not another word about this whole foolish business, right?"

"*What* foolish business?" he deadpanned, and they both laughed. "I think I hear a sick airplane wing calling me. See you around, boss." He kissed his mother on the cheek and walked out of the house.

His grandfather had told Grant his own philosophy once long ago: "If something is wrong, son, do what you can to make it right. But if there is nothing you can do about it, grit your teeth and go on to something else!"

Right now that seemed good advice. There was plenty else to go on to, starting with the ripped fabric on the underside of the Citabria's right wing tip. A woman student had tangled with cholla cactus when she landed short and was

46

so shaken she lost control and ground-looped. A patch and a can of blue spray paint would take care of the damage, Grant hoped as he entered the hangar.

It was decided Grant would spend both Saturday and Sunday at the sailplane field in Tucson. He had been planning to work at the airport on Saturday, but his mother felt he needed another flight or two in the BG before entering a contest.

"I want you to do well, even if this contest is your first," she said. "You go out there Saturday and get a few more hours in the BG. Then maybe you won't land out. Okay?"

"You really know how to hurt a guy, Mom," Grant said, but he was grinning. "If you insist, I'll trailer over Saturday morning. You're sure you can run things here?"

"Probably not the way you could, Captain Super," she teased. "But I have an idea the airport will still be functioning when you come back. The real question is, can you fly in the contest without *our* help?"

"Sure, Mom. I can always find somebody to help me put the wings on, and that's about all there is to do on the bird."

"How about a crew to follow you with the trailer?"

"No problem. There's always somebody eager for the chance. I don't know why, though," he admitted. "It's sure not like flying."

"Don't knock it," his mother advised. "Just go out there and prove we didn't spend all those hours in vain. I want to see that Class B trophy on our bookcase when summer ends."

"Always the pressure," Grant said. "You make a space for it and promise to keep it dusted. I'll win it."

"Deal!" his mother said, putting out her hand to seal the bargain. "Now get out there and do two days' work today, so we can spare you for the weekend."

47

He did the two days' work, finishing after dark by spraying another coat of paint on the Citabria wing by lamplight and finally getting the muffler and tail pipe on the pickup. He couldn't ask someone to crew for him in a truck that wasn't legal. His mother brought his supper out to the hangar, and he ate in hurried bites between jobs.

Then, unlocking the BG's trailer, he opened the rear door and rolled the fuselage out so he could work on the rudder cables. The test flight had indicated that the pedals were slightly off-center, and he adjusted them with the turnbuckles. Then he spread a damp cloth on the floorboards and took a file to the sharp aluminum angles the bearded man had gashed himself on. With luck, he thought, the guy might get lockjaw for his trouble.

Sobering, Grant hoped sincerely that he would never see any of the trio again. Already, as he began to get excited about the contest, the trouble began to fade from his mind. He was putting the fuselage back in the trailer, carefully easing it along the track, when his mother came out to ask when he'd be coming in.

"Contest winners need their rest," she warned. "It's past twelve, Grant, and you said you have to get up early."

"That was for Sunday," he corrected her. "No big rush in the morning. It'll only take me about an hour to drive to Ryan Field, and the thermals won't be working before eleven o'clock or so. Hold the noise down when you get up in the morning, will you?"

"You rascal," she said, rapping him on the head with the book she was carrying. "Close the hangar doors and get to bed."

Sleep was slow coming, but it was great to lie there in the quiet darkness and plan how he would fly the contest. If the day was good, and it probably would be, the Class B task would be to fly 150 miles or more. The sleek fiberglass superships in Class A might be sent out on a triangle total-

48

ing 200 miles or more. Last year the longest A task had been just over Diamond distance, some 315 miles, all the way to Prescott, Wickenburg, and return.

Grant grinned at the ceiling thinking of such a cross-country flight, with no engine up front. As Harry said, it did seem like magic, as if the plane were aided by some sort of aerial leprechaun.

There should be about half a dozen ships in Class B. The club's two-place Blanik would be entered, along with the K-6 single-place wood-and-fabric ship that had won the event last year and had also earned several of the club pilots their Diamond Distance badges. Two all-metal HP-11's and a 1-34 from Phoenix were supposed to be coming down, plus an LP-49 home-built from Douglas. But Grant thought he had the edge.

It must have been nearly two o'clock when he finally got his eyes shut and drifted off to sleep. Later he was roused by a noise and then decided he had dreamed it. Vaguely he heard a car passing on the highway, and then at last he slept soundly, not to wake until his mother called him next morning.

At first it seemed like part of his long, involved dream about the contest. Through bleary eyes he looked across the foot of his bed to hear her excitedly ask him what he had done with the BG.

"The BG?" he mumbled, still half out of it. "What did I—"

"It's not in the hangar, Grant!" his mother said excitedly, and he knew this was no dream. "Your sailplane is gone, trailer and all. Did you take it somewhere before you came to bed last night? The hangar doors weren't locked."

"You're kidding!" Grant shouted, awake all the way now. He flung back the covers and scrambled out of bed. In his pajamas, he raced out of the house and across the grass toward the hangar. No one was about this early in the morning, but it would have made little difference if all his students had been there gawking at him. The BG *couldn't* be gone! He had locked it up in the trailer last night and—

Then suddenly Grant remembered vaguely hearing a noise and a car driving down the highway. Had he forgotten to lock up? he wondered as he entered the hangar.

His mother was right. The trailer was gone from its place by the tool locker. He groaned and looked around desperately to be sure it hadn't just been moved to some unaccustomed place. Maybe it had been in Harry's way. But Harry never came to work this early on a Saturday.

"I've looked everywhere," his mother said. She was already dressed in slacks and shirt, ready for the busy day's work. Grant took her wrist to look at the time. It was a quarter to eight. "I was hoping when I missed it that you had gotten up early and gone to the glider field," she added, concern in her eyes. "Could some of your friends be playing a joke?"

"With jokes like that I wouldn't need any enemies," Grant said tightly.

Still hoping, he searched the ground for traces of the trailer's tracks, but found nothing. Anyway, he was no Indian tracker. Four bits an hour, his comedian friends had kidded him about his labor on the sailplane. Now it looked as if he were going to get zilch, even before he could fly in one contest.

"I'd better call the sheriff, Grant," his mother said, turning toward the office. "It'll be pretty hard to hide a trailer that big for very long."

Her words offered a ray of hope. An airplane was easy to steal; you just climbed in and took off. But a sailplane was more of a problem. That was really what made it so crazy. Who would steal a sailplane?

50

While his mother got on the phone, Grant hurried back to the house to get dressed. By the time he had finished, she was back with the word that a deputy would be out shortly to check on the theft.

"I gave him a description of the trailer, Grant, and he said they'd broadcast it immediately. That might help. Can you eat some breakfast?"

"Maybe a cup of coffee," he said. "But I couldn't get any food down, Mom. Thanks anyway. Is it okay if I take the 182 and go looking? I can't stand around and worry."

"Of course," she said, nodding sympathetically. "If I hear anything, I'll call you. Don't worry about your students. Somebody can fill in for you."

"Thanks, Mom. You're the greatest," he told her. Then he headed for the big green Cessna that had been their meal ticket for so long.

Ten minutes later he had fueled it, preflighted it, and made a fast takeoff that ended five thousand feet above the ground. Then, for two discouraging hours, he patrolled the surrounding country, fanning out in an expanding search pattern that showed him hundreds of square miles. Twice he thought he had spotted the trailer. Once he was so sure that he let out a yell and reached for the mike dangling above the sun visor, but each time he was mistaken. The first suspect was a monstrously long horse trailer; the other, a home-built utility box that didn't even have a roof when he buzzed it for a better look.

At ten fifteen he was almost ready to give up, but he decided to make one more pattern, moving out another five miles with his search. His mother's voice on the radio broke that off just as he started.

"Cessna Four-Five-Five-One-George, this is Stone Field Unicom. Over."

"Five-One-George. Go ahead, Stone."

51

"Grant, you just had a phone call," his mother said. He could feel her agitation, even through the transmitter, forty miles of sky, and the rattly speaker in the 182. "It was that man—Reese."

"Reese?" he repeated, unbelievingly. "What did he want, Mom?"

"He wouldn't say. Do you want me to call the sheriff again? This whole thing—"

"Mom!" he almost shouted. "Don't call anybody! Did he leave a number?"

"Yes," she came back. "But—"

"Sit tight," Grant told her sharply. "Don't call anybody. I'll be back in fifteen minutes. Five-One-George out."

Already he had wrapped the plane around in a diving turn. Burning off five hundred feet a minute, he put the nose on a line with Stone Field and watched the airspeed climb to the red line. He was tempted to exceed it, but he held back. He needed another minute to think, anyway. Why hadn't he thought about the three mysterious men right away?

At the field he had to force himself to ease patiently into the pattern in back of a Cessna 150 shooting landings. Flying slowly, he kept well behind and made a routine landing, cut off at the first taxiway, and practically flew into the hangar. His mother was waiting when he shut down the engine and opened the door.

"Here's the number," she said, waving a sheet of paper as he vaulted out. "I'm going to listen on the other phone, Grant."

"Mom," he said firmly. "Don't do it. Okay? Let's not give anybody an excuse to make trouble. Please?"

"I'm afraid," she said in a trembling voice. "I'm afraid for you, Grant. Please be careful."

"They can't shoot me over the phone, can they?" he

shouted back as he ran for the office. "Give me five minutes privacy."

It was a Tucson number, and he fidgeted impatiently through the formalities with the operator. Then he heard the crisp, pleasant voice of Reese, as nonchalant as if the man were just calling to chat.

"Grant? Thanks for answering so promptly. I'm calling about your sailplane—"

"Great," Grant cut in. "I've been trying to find it all morning. It's been stolen."

"I know," Reese said patiently. "Secondhand, that is. Those two clowns must have their brains in their shoes. Grant, I'm sorry. I apologized before for all this ridiculous confusion. Now I'm downright embarrassed."

"Big deal," Grant said bitterly. "I'm out a five-thousand-dollar bird and you're embarrassed."

"I don't blame you for being uptight," Reese said. "But I have good news for you. I can take you to your sailplane if you'll trust me."

"You can?" Grant shouted. "Why didn't you say that first, and I wouldn't have blown my stack. What do I do?"

"There's an independent filling station near the junction of Interstate Ten and the Benson Highway. Drive there and park in the back. Come alone, and I'll pick you up shortly after you get there. You should be able to make it in . . . about an hour, right?"

"Right," Grant said tensely. "But where's my BG? And why all this Mickey Mouse mystery stuff?"

"Sorry about that," Reese said, good-naturedly. "I'm in a funny position, Grant, and things don't always go the way I want them to. But I'm on the level when I say I can take you right to your ship. It's unharmed, and you'll have no problems if you follow instructions. Okay?"

"I . . . guess so," Grant admitted. He was confused, but

53

he was hopeful too. And that made the big difference. Maybe he could still make the contest.

"Good. I'll see you in an hour then. Alone." And the phone clicked down.

Grant licked his lips and cleared his throat. With relief he opened the door and saw his mother across the hangar talking with Harry. She hadn't tried to eavesdrop, and Grant admired her for that, knowing how big the temptation must have been.

"What did you find out?" she called while he was still several yards away. Harry looked curious too, and Grant knew his mother had clued him in on the mysterious phone call.

"He says he can take me to the BG. That it's okay, and I'm in no danger. He apologized again for the two gorillas. How's that for a piece of good news?"

"Wonderful," his mother said, clasping her hands in a little gesture of delight. "It's an answer to a prayer, isn't it, Harry?"

"Right, Flo," the mechanic said. "But what's the catch, Grant? You have to pay this guy a ransom, or what?"

"He didn't say anything about that. Just for me to meet him in Tucson, and—"

"Let's go," Harry said. "Flo, you're going to be short-handed today, but we've got to clear this thing up."

"No deal," Grant said bluntly, shaking his head. "Reese said to come alone, or he doesn't show. That's the way I have to play it. I've got to get my ship back."

"I wouldn't let you risk your life, even for a Learjet," his mother protested. "Grant, listen to me—"

"*You* listen, Mom," he said patiently. "We've kept our mouths shut as per the bargain. Right? If they do anything to me, they know that you know where I am, and who I'm with. If this guy Reese were just out to get me, he could do it right here at the airport. They took the BG. I guess they could have wiped us both out if they had wanted to."

"But you don't know a thing about this man Reese," his mother protested.

"I don't," Grant admitted. "But he sure shows me a lot more than his two hippie sidekicks. I've got a crazy notion that they're not all on the same team. Mom, I think this is going to work, so let me play it my way. Okay?"

"Oh, my," his mother said weakly. "Harry?"

"Let him go," the mechanic said, spreading his hands. "He can take care of himself."

"Thanks," Grant said gratefully. "You look out for Mom, Harry."

"I'll do that. Any clown who gets out of line will have to eat a monkey wrench or get his hair parted with a sledge hammer," Harry promised with a fierce frown.

"I'm taking the pickup," Grant said. "I'm supposed to meet this guy in an hour, so I'll have to hurry. Don't get any cops-and-robbers ideas about trailing me in the plane. We're amateurs at that stuff, so forget it. I'll see you soon— *with* the BG if all goes well."

"I pray that it does, dear," his mother said softly, and she hugged him before he left.

He knew the gas station Reese had mentioned, and drove right to it, pulling into one of the parking spaces behind it just fifty-two minutes after he left the airport. His heart was beating so hard that he was aware of its hammering, but he made himself sit there and wait. A minute later he caught a motion in his rearview mirror and stiffened in the seat, but it was only one of the attendants.

"Need anything, buddy?" the man asked curiously.

"No," Grant said. "Just taking a break, if it's okay."

"Sure," the attendant said, shrugging. He went back into the station, and Grant tried to relax. It was a tough job.

Reese showed on schedule, five minutes after Grant. He pulled the black Ford into the stall next to Grant and motioned for him to come over.

Taking a deep breath, Grant climbed down from the pickup and got into the other car, glancing around to see if anyone had noticed. There seemed to be nobody watching. He was on his own, unless Harry or his mother was peeking from a nearby telephone pole. Grant hoped they weren't.

"You're right on the dot, Grant," Reese said. In the daytime he looked even more friendly. About forty, Grant guessed, slender and sandy-haired, the hair cut shorter than most men wore it.

"The BG," Grant said, wasting no time. "I'm eager to get it back. I'm sorry about dropping in on that strip again. I goofed. But I haven't mentioned anything to anybody."

"Good," Reese said, nodding soberly. "I'm sorry, too, Grant, and I apologize for this grossness on the part of my friends. But I think we can set things right. Are you ready to go get your sailplane?"

"I didn't drive this far just to buy gas," Grant said, forcing a grin. "Where is the BG?"

"It's in Mexico. Let's go." As Grant tried to field that one, Reese turned the key and started his engine.

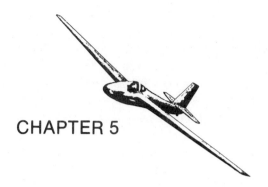

CHAPTER 5

Grant could tell what speed limit was posted on the highway signs that flicked past by simply glancing at the speedometer on the Ford's instrument panel. Reese drove by the book, far differently from the way he had that night on the rutted dirt road. And all the time he kept up a running conversation, mostly about the BG and Grant's plans for the contest.

"No reason why you can't fly tomorrow," he said optimistically. "Your bird should be safely back before dark tonight."

They crossed the border at Nogales with no trouble and drove on into Mexico. A few miles south, Reese swung off the pavement and headed west on a gravel road. Grant had been in Nogales, Mexico, a number of times; but he had no idea where they were headed, and Reese would give no specific answers to his questions. Without making it obvious, Grant had noted the odometer reading at the border, hoping that he could keep track roughly of where they were. But the road wound lazily through barren, deserted hills, and only once did Grant see any sign of life, a tiny adobe shack to the north of the road.

It was almost a quarter past three when Reese swerved

sharply to pick up a pair of bumpy ruts angling to the left from the gravel road. "We're almost there," he said.

Grant frowned. The trail led toward a low range of hills south of them, but there was no sign of a trailer or sailplane. There wasn't much of anything but cactus and brush, plus an occasional hawk or buzzard swooping effortlessly on lift from the ridge. If the BG was down here at the end of this road, it might have been shaken apart by the rutted, washed-out trail.

The grim thought suddenly crossed his mind that there might be nothing on the other side of the hills but a bullet, which would get rid of him as a witness to some kind of criminal operation. He had told himself that Reese was different from his two friends in more than appearance, but that might be a vain hope. He had seen pictures of brutal killers who could have passed for kindergarten teachers.

He had begun to wish he had taken the little pistol out of his mother's desk drawer and hidden it under his shirt somehow, when they topped the last rise and he looked down into the long valley on the other side. The shock of seeing the familiar white shape of the BG was so great that he shouted out loud and brought his hand down sharply on the panel in front of him.

"There it is!" he yelled exultantly. "That's my BG!"

"That's what we came for," Reese said, grinning. "Feel better now?"

"A lot better," Grant admitted, but then his forehead creased as he saw the drab-looking Cessna 150 beyond the sailplane. It suddenly hit him that the BG was assembled, and that the trailer was nowhere in sight.

Reese slid to a fast stop abreast of the sailplane and climbed out. Grant went pounding across the intervening brush-covered soil toward his pride and joy, grabbing the wing as soon as he reached it and running his hands along the leading edge to assure himself that the sailplane was all right. Moving to the other wing tip, he rocked it up and down. It felt solid, and so did the tail when he checked that. When he untied the cloth canopy cover and took it off, the cockpit looked as shipshape as he had left it the night before.

"Does she pass inspection?" Reese asked. He leaned against the wing across the fuselage from Grant and took out a pack of cigarettes.

"Looks good," Grant admitted happily, refusing the proffered cigarette. He unlatched the canopy and gently set it on the ground. Moving the stick, he watched the corresponding motions of elevator and ailerons, nodding in relief. The flap handle worked too, dropping the wide flaps steeply from the rear of the wing. Climbing in, he got his feet on the rudder pedals and checked them, craning his neck to see the big rudder swing in answer.

"Okay," he said. "Everything seems to work, but where is the trailer?" Now that the most pressing question was answered, there were others that had to be taken care of.

"I'll have to guess with you," Reese said, blowing a long tendril of smoke down the wind. "But it should be waiting for you when you get back to the field."

"Back to the field?" Grant repeated in amazement. "What do I do, *carry* this sailplane home?"

"It would probably be easier to fly it," Reese said around his cigarette. "And a lot more fun, I'd think."

"You've got to be kidding," Grant said, staring at the man. "Flying across the border without clearance is illegal. Besides, I'd need a tow to get into the air. Remember?"

"I remember," Reese said, grinning. "It just happens that the airplane over yonder has a tow hook, and I believe there's two hundred feet of quarter-inch nylon rope in the cockpit. With two rings attached."

"I'm dreaming this whole thing," Grant said, leaning

weakly against the leading edge and staring at the Cessna. There was indeed a tow hook protruding from the plane's fuselage just behind the tail wheel. "Don't tell me you're checked out as a tow pilot?"

"I'm checked out to do a lot of things," Reese admitted, his face expressionless. Dropping the cigarette, he ground it out with a boot heel and then looked at Grant. "Now about the illegality of crossing the Mexican-American border without going through a port of entry."

"I don't want to lose my license," Grant protested. "It would be a lot better to trailer back across."

"But you have no idea how difficult that would be," Reese told him, a faint smile crossing his face.

"Somebody pulled it down here," Grant retorted. "Roads run both directions."

"Not in this case," Reese said apologetically. "Look, Grant, I'm sorry for what must seem . . . Mickey Mouse to you. But believe me, flying out is the simplest way of doing it. Don't tell me glider guiders never accidentally drift onto this side of the line."

"Well," Grant hedged, "I haven't." But Reese was right, of course. There wasn't any dotted line marked out on the barren terrain to match the international border on the map. It *was* easy to wander off course, especially when you were scratching to find lift and stay airborne.

"So who's to know where you took off? I tow you up, and you release and grab a thermal. From there you're home free in an hour or so, and tomorrow you go win that contest."

"I don't know," Grant said. His stomach was bothering him now, queasy from nerves. "There's the Border Patrol, and I hear that Air Defense Command monitors the line with radar."

"No problem from the Border Patrol," Reese said. "And if an ADC scanner did pick up the BG by some miracle,

60

what can they do to a young pilot who just happened to stray a little bit in his home-built sailplane? Grant, you don't have much choice, and we don't have all afternoon. Look over there!"

He swung his arm suddenly to the west, and Grant turned to see the big dust devil slanting across the desert toward them. The funnel must have been fifty feet in diameter, and not just dust but pieces of brush were spiraling strongly upward. It was a booming day for soaring.

"Okay," he said at last, fighting down the feeling the decision brought. He had heard of planes being caught south of the border and never making it back. Customs could be sticky. And how did you explain a fifty-foot sailplane to the authorities?

"Good show," Reese said, a broad smile softening the planes of his lean face. "You point this baby the way you want to go, and I'll fire up the towplane." He trotted off toward the Cessna.

Grant checked the wind and turned the BG slightly to the right. The Cessna's engine caught, died, then sputtered and coughed back to life. As it trundled around in a sweeping 180-degree arc, Grant set the right wing of the BG down and watched Reese swing into position a hundred feet ahead. Engine idling, the Cessna's door flipped open, and Reese left it at a run, a coil of yellow nylon looped over his left arm.

"Hop in," he yelled, and Grant climbed into the BG's cockpit, snugging the chute straps and then the harness. Reese set the canopy in place over him, and Grant latched it securely. The temperature inside the BG's cockpit began to rise immediately, and Grant was glad for the sliding vent in the left side of the canopy. He opened it wide and then grabbed the tow release as Reese bent to hook him up.

"Check it!" Reese ordered, and Grant yanked the lever.

The rope popped free and the tall man nodded approval. Then he hooked it up again.

"All set?" Reese asked him, squatting alongside the cockpit. Grant gave him a thumb-up okay sign. He knew he must look as tense as he felt.

"Relax," the man told him, grinning. "As soon as I get the slack out, we go. Get your right wing up fast. And have a nice flight."

Grant nodded and watched his tow pilot jog back to the waiting plane. He was glad now that he had practiced unassisted takeoffs. The brush might have been a problem otherwise. Up ahead, the Cessna inched forward, tugging the looping rope through the sandy soil. Once the nylon snagged on a clump of brush, and Grant held his breath until it pulled free and straightened. At last the line was taut, clear of the ground and tugging the BG's nose.

He had purposely angled the sailplane to the right, and now he held left stick and full left rudder as the pull of the towline pivoted the sailplane to the left. The right wing came up smartly with its sudden speed, and Grant nodded his satisfaction. He was rolling now, slowly at first in the soft terrain, but picking up speed quickly. At 30 knots he had the craft balanced on its wheel; at 35 knots he lifted gently off the ground and exhaled with relief. So far so good.

The thick cone of dust from the Cessna's prop hit him then, and for several exciting seconds he flew blind. But when he could see again, the Cessna had cleared the ground and was beginning its climb. Gentle on the controls, Grant followed the towplane up and up, keeping its wings on the horizon and the BG's nose aimed straight at the Cessna's cabin. In position, he took a quick look around for other aircraft, then swept his eyes across the terrain below. Nothing in sight moved, and again he whistled his breath out.

He looked back at the towplane in time to catch it drifting to his left. Correcting smoothly, he got in position and checked his altimeter.

He had planned to tow to two thousand feet to be sure, but Reese made it unnecessary. The dust devil they had seen earlier was still alive, and the Cessna towed Grant straight for it. About fifteen hundred feet above the ground, the plane banked at the last second to avoid the vertically rushing funnel of hot air. Leaning quickly forward, Grant pulled hard on the release, and felt and heard the metallic snap. He could see the rope falling away from the nose just as the edge of the thermal slammed his wing upward. It was a delicious feeling, and at once the variometer began its shrill, happy squeal.

At 3:52 Grant released, fifteen hundred feet above the ground. At 4:01 he rolled out of the booming thermal and headed north, his altimeter reading a lovely 11,700 feet. He had averaged better than 1100 feet a minute up for nine minutes. All he had to do now was fall out of the sky onto Stone Field. The thought made him squeeze the mike switch and begin a radio call.

"Stone Unicom, this is Briegleb sailplane Eight-Eight-Hotel. Over." He must have been talking into a dead mike. Twisting as far as he could, he reached back and checked the battery plug. It was in, and he had all the switches on. But there was still no response from the radio on any of the channels. Grimly he figured out why and said some harsh things about the idiots who had stolen the BG. Then he shrugged, knowing it was a detail. He would be home in three quarters of an hour and could tell them firsthand.

The first milestone was crossing the border, and Grant estimated he was back in the United States ten minutes after leaving the thermal. Twenty miles to the east, Nogales slid under his right wing. Breathing easier in spite of the altitude, he swung the nose from its line on Keystone Peak and set up a heading that should carry him home. It was obvious by now that there was strong lift all over the sky. He kicked up his speed to 70 knots, and then 80. *Fly like this tomorrow, chum, and you have the contest won,* he told himself excitedly.

He could see the X of their two runways now, ahead and far below. Much as he hated to kill altitude that way, he added flaps and pointed the nose straight at the field. There was no traffic at the moment, and he entered the pattern at eight hundred feet, still flying fast. He landed with a grin that touched both his ears, and his roll ended near the hangar, where his mother, Harry, and several others waited for him. His mother caught the wing before it could drop, then lifted the canopy off—and embarrassed him by kissing him right there in front of everybody.

"Grant, I'm so thankful! You're all right?" she asked as she finally let him go. Harry was grinning, enjoying Grant's discomfort and looking relieved too.

"Sure, I'm all right, Mom," Grant said. "And so is the BG. Except for the radio. Sorry I couldn't call and let you know sooner."

"I was so worried," his mother said, as they pulled the sailplane toward the hangar doors. "It was all I could do to keep from calling the sheriff again. I guess we should call now, shouldn't we? Now that the BG is safe."

"As soon as the trailer is returned," Grant said, frowning. Reese had told him it would be here, but he saw no sign of it.

"The trailer?" his mother asked, the fact just then dawning on her that it was missing. "But where did you find the sailplane? And how—"

"Let's go in the office, Mom," he told her, not wanting to talk too much in front of the strangers clustered near. "Harry, can you handle the BG?"

The mechanic nodded, and Grant took his mother by the arm and walked her quickly to the office. With the door closed, he sat on the desk and told her the whole weird story, from meeting Reese at the filling station to catching the strong thermal fifteen miles south of the border. She listened in amazement, eyes wide, her mouth open in disbelief.

"They must have driven across the border somewhere out in the desert," she said, shaking her head in confusion. "Didn't Reese explain anything?"

"He couldn't," Grant said tightly. "Or he wouldn't. He did say the trailer would be returned. In fact, it was supposed to be here."

"We haven't seen it," his mother told him. "There's been no word from the sheriff's office either. But at least we have the BG back. That's the important part!"

"Right," Grant said. "Look, what can I do to help around here now? I've just about killed the last couple of days causing nothing but trouble. Any student hops left?"

"There are two waiting. But when I told them you were trying to find the stolen glider, they were sympathetic. I'm sure they wouldn't mind coming back some other time."

"No need," Grant said, moving to the door. "Maybe it will help me unwind. It has been a . . . tight day."

"Unwind in the instructor's seat?" she teased. "That's not the way I remember it. Oh, it's so wonderful to have you back. You *and* the BG!"

"Right," he agreed over his shoulder as he walked across the concrete floor. "Who's up next in the 150? Let's get into the blue."

His student, for all his eight hours of instruction, still had a tendency to fly with the left wing low and a compensating yaw to the right. But it did help Grant unwind and get his mind off the tension after the risky flight in the sailplane.

He even suggested an extra takeoff and go-around for good measure and made the student realize he was standing on the rudder pedal without knowing it. Even the landing was better, and the man left the field looking as delighted as if he had already soloed.

The sun was an hour off the horizon when Grant pushed the Cessna into its tie-down area and looped the chains through the wing fittings. Quite suddenly he realized that he was starving, and with a grin he headed for the house. It would be an hour or so till supper, but he could grab a sandwich and a tall glass of milk to keep him going.

His mother was in the kitchen already taking the meat out of the refrigerator. She smiled and asked if his student had gotten the kinks out.

"I think so," Grant said, grinning. "Anyway, he's getting the idea that he doesn't have to help the plane quite so much just to fly straight and level."

"Hadn't we better call the sheriff?" she asked, changing the subject abruptly.

"Mom, I don't know," he said uncertainly. "I wish that trailer would show up. It's going to be rough getting to the contest if it doesn't."

"I could tow you over with the 182," she offered. "Then just don't land out, and you won't need a crew."

"Thanks for the vote of confidence," he said, opening the refrigerator. "Look, if we don't hear something by—"

The insistent honking of a horn cut him off, and he went to the window frowning. Probably some tourist trying to find the way to Tucson, he thought, and then he caught his breath. The BG trailer was parked on the hangar apron, riding a hitch on the black Ford.

With a shout, Grant raced from the house. The second jolt came when he saw it wasn't Reese at the wheel, but the fat bearded man. His buddy sat alongside him, and they both eyed Grant with hostility.

"Sorry we're a little late," the driver said in a tone that belied any apology. "We've got our own private port of entry on the border, but we had to wait for the right moment. Did you get your glider back in one piece?"

"It's inside," Grant said.

"That's nice," the driver said. "Isn't that nice?" he asked his partner.

"Better than nice," the man agreed, almost smiling. "Let's go see for ourselves."

"You don't have to," Grant told them, moving toward the back of the car. "Just help me lift the trailer off the hitch—"

"Don't tell us, kid," the driver said, climbing out. "We tell you, remember? Now, lead us to your great white bird."

Grant's stomach started tightening again. As he headed into the hangar, he saw his mother coming across the blacktop toward them, and waved her back.

"You'll let supper burn!" he warned. "Everything's okay, Mom. Go on back to the kitchen." With relief he saw her pause uncertainly, nod, and then turn back to the house.

The three of them reached the BG together, and before Grant could protest, the smaller man had reached in through the vent and unlatched the canopy. He did it expertly, and a moment later had lifted the parachute out and removed the seat back.

"You did another nice thing," he said. "No more sharp edges. I didn't cut my hand this time." While Grant watched in confusion, the man reached far back into the storage area over the wheel well, and when he straightened up, he had a small package in his hand. Hefting it, he looked toward his partner with a grin. And the other man was snapping pictures with a small camera!

"You can't beat air freight," he said. "Thanks, kid. That was a nice run you made this afternoon. Now you're one of us mules!"

"What's in that package?" Grant demanded. He was afraid he already knew what it was.

"You're a bright kid," the driver said, slipping the packet into his shirt as his partner replaced the panel. "Figure it out yourself. And while you're at it, check the rap for transporting H across the border."

"Wait a minute!" Grant cried. "I didn't do anything but fly my sailplane back. You can't—"

"Sorry, kid, we got witnesses. Three of us, to just one of you. So when you get the urge to call your local sheriff, better think about it. Okay?" The two men started for the door.

"Hold it!" Grant yelled, moving after them.

"We can't wait, kid. Have to keep the stuff moving, you know. But we'll be in touch." While Grant stood there in sick fury, they disconnected the trailer, got into the Ford, and raced out onto the highway.

Oh, boy, Grant told himself. *You're in it now. You're really in it now!*

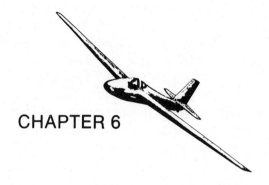

CHAPTER 6

It seemed to Grant he hardly slept that night, worrying about what had happened the day before. And always his mind kept circling back to the ugly fact that he and the BG had actually been part of a smuggling operation. Worst of all, heroin smuggling. When trouble first threatened, he should have insisted that his mother leave Arizona for safety back east. Somehow he could have gotten word to the state's narcotics people, or even the FBI. Sure, there would have been risk, but he would not have locked *himself* into the mess!

He couldn't change what had happened for all his worrying over it. He was in deep trouble now, and there seemed no way to get out. His personal world had turned rotten almost overnight. Bitterly he wondered why he should think he could escape the general rottenness that seemed to infect everything.

He was up shortly after six, and as quickly as he could, he went out to the hangar and unlocked the big doors. With relief he saw that the BG was still there, apparently untouched since Harry had rolled it into the corner. The trailer was there too, and Grant angled it around by muscle power until it was in position for him to load the sailplane.

He remembered the ailing radio and did a quick check. The problem wasn't hard to find—a battery wire had been yanked from its terminal. An accident, or to keep him from communicating? While he tried to decide, Grant got a soldering iron and put the battery lead back on. Everything else checked out all right. He couldn't handle the wing disassembly by himself, but he did what he could until Harry showed up. Then the two of them completed the job of getting the BG into the trailer in about fifteen minutes.

"Hey, I'm sure glad we got the ship back in time for you to enter the contest," Harry said as they locked the trailer door. "You place high now, you hear?"

"Right," Grant said, forcing a smile. He had little heart for soaring now, with worry weighting his shoulders like a lead cast. But what else was there to do? He couldn't let them know what the real situation was. He'd have to go out there to Ryan Field and go through the motions. Another flight might help ease his soul sickness. He might even come up with some kind of a solution. But he feared that would take a miracle.

He ate breakfast with his mother, and then they drove the few miles to church. Grant heard little of the sermon and had to force himself to sing the words in the hymnal. But he prayed harder than he could ever remember praying. If anyone needed help, it was Grant Stone, and that help was apparently going to have to come from other than human hands.

He got on the road just before ten, his mother kissing him for good luck and Harry shaking his hand firmly and repeating his request for Grant to win big. The trip to Ryan took about an hour, and he got to the pilot's meeting only a few minutes late. The contest task was on the blackboard: Class A and Class B would fly from Ryan Field to Douglas-

Bisbee International, to Nogales International, and return to Ryan. Grant whistled under his breath. That was more than 230 miles. The contest director must be expecting a booming day!

Surprisingly, a tingle of honest excitement went through Grant as he listened to the weather briefing and studied the faces of his competition. Then it was time to take a number from the contest director's battered old hat and select a takeoff time. Grant drew number four and got a takeoff slot of 12:14. With such a long task he was going to have to hurry to be ready. Picking up his film and landing card, he headed for the trailer at a run.

As he had hoped, there was plenty of volunteer help, and he got the BG assembled and the wings taped by 11:45. Then there was barely time to mark his course on the Phoenix Sectional Chart, grab a quick sandwich at the snack wagon, and fill his canteen with ice water. Slipping into his parachute, he helped Billy Tabor, his hastily acquired crew chief, roll the ship into its position in the long line of sailplanes. Then he eased into the cockpit. It had all happened so fast he had to sit there and catch his breath. He had briefly considered declaring the task to be an attempt at his Gold Badge, but there wasn't enough time.

"You going to head for Rincon Peak?" Billy asked, crouching over the cockpit to shade Grant as they waited. "Beautiful buildup of cumulus clouds over there."

"I don't think so, Billy," Grant said, his excitement growing in a way he hadn't hoped for. "If I can get any decent lift near the field, I'll head straight out. The Whetstone Mountains are just about on course, and I can work the lift over them."

"Makes sense." Billy nodded. "Sounds like a fantastic day. Too bad you haven't got oxygen."

71

"I'm lucky to have a ship at all," Grant said soberly.

"What a ship, though!" Billy said enthusiastically. "You did a great job on it. Lots of luck."

He slapped Grant on the shoulder, and then it was time to snap an identification photo with the camera mounted on the left side of the cockpit. The line chief jogged up with the towrope, and Grant pulled the release. They checked it, hooked him up again, and Grant gave a thumb-up ready signal to the man at his wing tip.

The wing came up, and Grant took a deep breath as he watched the towplane begin to straighten the towline that snaked across the narrow runway. It was a Super Cub. He would get a fast ride up.

The rudder of the towplane began to waggle the instant the rope tightened, and Grant worked his own rudder pedals to show that he was ready to go. The rising roar of 180 horsepower in the Super Cub came back to him on the slipstream as the BG inched forward and then accelerated quickly. Grant balanced the sailplane on its wheel and steered precisely down the white-painted center line. He quickly left his wing runner behind, and the BG floated upward.

Grant held about five feet off the runway, dropping his left wing slightly into the quartering breeze, and watched the towplane rocket into the blue. After that it was just a matter of hanging on and gaining altitude. The rapid ascent could fool you into thinking you were in a thermal, so he played it smart and hung on all the way to two thousand feet, the legal maximum. With the towplane flying level, he could accurately read lift.

Over the drop zone his variometer squealed, and Grant felt his right wing go up. With a quick movement he released and banked tightly into the lift, his face breaking

72

into a broad grin as the needle nudged 400 feet a minute up. It was going to be a great day!

Five minutes later he left the thermal, in good position and high enough to make his start. For the first time he used his recently assigned contest number, GS. "Start gate, this is George Sierra, one mile out."

"Roger, George Sierra," came the answer. "We have you in sight."

He had the stick well forward now, and the BG quivered at red-line speed as he dived for the imaginary gate 3300 feet above the start line. He could be no higher than that altitude for an official start. The closer to it, and the faster he flew, the better.

"George Sierra, Mark!" came the voice on the radio. Then, "Good start, George Sierra."

"Roger, thank you," Grant acknowledged. Shaking with excitement, he eased back on the stick and settled himself in the seat. His first contest start had been right out of the book, and he regained five hundred precious feet, leveling off at about 3800 feet above the ground. The radio crackled as One-Tango called from the IP. That would be a Nimbus, one of the big Open-Class birds. Grant was glad he didn't have to compete with those super ships and their fantastic 48-to-1 glide angle.

Several contestants had played it safe and headed for the ridge a few miles east to work weak ridge lift and thermals before setting out on course. Grant cruised at 50 knots for ten minutes without hitting a thing, and was beginning to think he should have done the same. Then he ran into a boomer, right over the gold dome of San Xavier Mission. It was better than the "house thermal" back at the drop zone, and he topped out under a beautiful cumulus cloud at 10,000 feet in just over seven minutes. *Keep it up, chum,*

73

and you may win this contest! he told himself joyfully. Trying to keep his voice matter-of-fact, he radioed his position to Billy Tabor.

Passing through several fair thermals without circling again, he reached the Whetstone Mountains, whose peaks were nearly 7700 feet. He caught a thermal going up at better than 1000 feet a minute and rolled out on course at twelve thousand. According to the book, he could average about 60 miles an hour in the BG with that kind of lift, and he was taut with excitement. Though he was still below the higher cloud base over the mountains, he told himself he wouldn't exceed twelve thousand feet without oxygen. And he wouldn't stay that high for long at a time.

Tombstone came in sight. There was a good strip there if he needed it, but something told him he wasn't going to need it. The day kept getting better, and when Billy Tabor radioed that he had reached Benson, Grant sent him on to Tombstone with instructions to stay there.

It was a storybook day, and he was flying as fast as 75 knots between thermals. With the slight tail wind, his ground speed was fantastic, and he couldn't believe how fast Tombstone slid by underneath and how quickly the huge Bisbee-Douglas Airport appeared. He took his turn-point photo from eleven thousand feet, pointing the BG's left wing tip at the center of the four long runways. Glancing at his watch, he did a quick estimate of his average speed for the first leg and came up with a fantastic 55 miles an hour. The fiberglass birds must be doing 80! As if reading his mind, a long-winged Nimbus slid by over him as he began the second leg. An arm raised in greeting, and Grant waved back, grinning broadly. This was living!

"George Sierra Ground, I'll race you to Nogales," he said into the mike. Most contest pilots used code for the turns and check points along the course, but Grant had decided to make all his calls in the clear.

"Roger, George Sierra," came Billy's elated voice. "Go, man, go!"

There should have been no sweat on the shorter second leg to Nogales. It was only about eighty miles, with at least nine airports along the way. Flying into the wind now, Grant decided to make his inter-thermal speed even faster, and at times it got as high as 80 knots as he raced from cloud to cloud. Speed steepened his glide angle drastically, but that was all right. The stronger the lift, the faster you could afford to fly between areas of lift. And today the lift was very strong.

He had decided he would try to stay between eight and twelve thousand feet. Even when he slid below eight thousand a time or two, he was unconcerned, for that still seemed like plenty of altitude—until he noticed how high the hills beneath him were and checked his map again. He whistled as he read the elevation of Bisbee airport—4780 feet. The BG was only about three thousand feet above the terrain in spite of the fat-looking 7800 on the altimeter!

But just then the BG hit a boomer of a thermal again, and shortly Grant was smiling down at Bisbee from twelve thousand feet. No sweat, he assured himself, and pushed the stick forward to hear the smooth rush of air over the wings and around the canopy at 80 knots. You didn't win contests floating along at a maximum glide speed of 50 knots.

Blasting along at 80 knots, Grant slid over Miller Peak with a hundred feet to spare. He was elated at being able to fly right on course instead of zigzagging all over the sky for lift. In spite of the head wind, he must have actually improved his ground speed a little. Another glass bird swept past him, five hundred feet higher and slightly south. The Mexican border was right down there. Grant tightened at the thought and tried to force it out of his mind.

He had seen no Class B sailplanes yet, and intended to keep it that way all around the course. Even as a fledgling sailplane pilot, he had adopted a philosophy about cross-country flying. A straight line was the shortest distance between two points, so why not fly that shortest distance? It was paying off on his first try. Several times he headed out into "blue holes" instead of angling off for a cumulus cloud to the right or left of his course line. Sure, he did a lot of careful breathing and thought *Up!* a lot, but a thermal always came along if he just kept pushing on.

With the Parker Canyon Lake strip in sight just ahead, Grant hit the first really heavy sink of the day. The variometer had been riding smoothly between 300 and 400 feet a minute down, when suddenly he began dropping 800 feet a minute. He could feel the sink, like an invisible hand shoving the BG toward the rocky terrain below. With a start he noticed that the airstrip was at an elevation of 5542, about eight hundred feet higher than Bisbee. He wet his lips nervously and began the throat-clearing bit. Billy Tabor picked that moment to call.

"George Sierra Ground at Sonoita," he said. "Where are you?"

"About even with you," Grant said, stalling a little. "Looks like a dead heat." Fifteen minutes later, when Billy called in from Patagonia, Grant was still only about ten miles west of the Parker Canyon Lake strip and wishing he had landed back there.

For nearly five minutes he had flown through the horrendous sink, unable to escape it no matter what he did. He thought of turning around, but by that time he was afraid

76

it would be even worse to backtrack through all that sub-siding air mass. With his altimeter quivering at six thousand feet above sea level, he finally blundered into some zero sink—not lift, but at least it wasn't driving him any lower.

"George Sierra," Billy called brightly. "I could cut off here and take the road to Tubac. That way I'll get back to Ryan Field in time to see you blaze across the finish line. Okay?"

Grant glanced at his map and understood his ground crew's reasoning. The cutoff would save Billy fifteen or twenty miles. But it would also put him farther away from the BG, and the BG might need him at any minute.

"Not okay," he replied reluctantly. "I have about suc-ceeded in flying the BG into the ground near Duquesne. Sorry about that. You better decide which is the fastest way to get here."

"Stay up, George Sierra!" Billy responded in dismay. "I'll be there as fast as I can. Keep me informed."

"Roger. George Sierra out."

It was a humbling experience. At twelve thousand feet he had been king of the hill, passing up lift unless it was better than 500 feet a minute. A thousand feet off the deck, he was humbly grateful for even zero sink. He cranked around in it for fully five minutes before he felt a wing bump upward slightly. Gingerly he turned toward the bubble and was rewarded by a feeble squeal from the audio part of the variometer.

For another several minutes Grant clung desperately to lift that was no better than 50 feet a minute. But the altimeter sluggishly climbed instead of sinking. Hardly breathing and straining upward with all his muscle and mind, he finally caught something better. A hundred feet a minute seemed like a boomer now, and it gave him courage

77

to explore a little more, letting the nose of the BG wander to sniff out stronger lift.

Gradually the 100 feet per minute became 200 and then 300. Grant realized how much he had been sweating and wiped at his face and neck with his left hand, not daring to take his right off the stick. The cluster of buildings along the dirt road and the mine openings in the mountain began to drop away. When Billy Tabor called again from the highway junction south of Nogales International, Grant was two thousand feet above the rocky foothills of the Patagonia Mountains, climbing now at better than 500 feet a minute.

"I have been saved by that happy sound you hear from the vario," he told his crew. "Hold where you are, and I'll send you home as fast as I can."

"Roger," Billy said, sounding relieved. "George Sierra Ground holding just south of Nogales Airport."

As the Patagonia Mountains dropped below him, Grant could imagine how a reprieved prisoner must feel. He could see beyond them at last, and there was the six-thousand-foot airstrip along the highway running northeast from the border city of Nogales. He had the BG locked tight in a booming thermal, and held it there until he hit thirteen thousand feet, momentarily waiving his twelve-thousand-foot rule. He wouldn't be long at that altitude, and he had enough experience to know danger signs if they came.

He snapped a picture of Nogales International from eleven thousand feet, then called Billy and sent him home with an apology for the delay.

"No problem," his crew assured him happily. "I think I just spotted you, by the way. You seem to have gotten airborne again."

"And does it feel good!" Grant assured him. "I was look-ing *up* at saguaro cactus not long ago."

He had learned something humbling about contest flying. Now instead of heading on a direct line for Ryan Field, as he would have done earlier, he angled off toward the 9500-foot crest of Mount Wrightson, due north of him. At the very least it would yield ridge lift, which would be unavailable over the flat terrain along the highway. Live and learn, he told himself. Fifteen minutes later his judgment paid off as he hit a boomer that nudged the vario up to 1200 feet a minute for part of his climb.

Now it was time to get out the final-glide calculator and decide how high to climb. To fly home at 80 knots, he would have to be a little more than ten thousand feet above the elevation of the finish gate. So he broke off the exhilarating climb at 12,500 above sea level and put the nose on the gleaming dome of San Xavier Mission. It seemed a long, long time since he had climbed above that landmark this morning, but when he checked his watch, he found he had been flying less than four hours. And if he hadn't goofed back there near Duquesne, he might be crossing the finish line by now.

The wind was from his left, not helping or hurting, and his ground speed was about 90 miles an hour. He covered the thirty-five miles of final glide in a hair over twenty-two minutes, feeling sorry for poor Billy Tabor, lagging far behind with the trailer. His ground crew would miss seeing Grant streak over the finish gate this time. But there would be other days, other tasks—he hoped.

Over San Xavier Mission he checked his altitude against the fifteen miles he had yet to go. Grinning, he eased the stick farther ahead, driving his speed up to 85 knots. Grabbing slightly to kill wind drift, he flew a head-on course for Ryan Field, coming down at an angle that would put him over the finish at about five hundred feet. He could drive faster and finish right on the deck the way some hot pilots did, but that was risky business, and he played it safe.

Three minutes later he squeezed the transmitter button

and spoke into the mike. "Ryan Finish Gate, this is George Sierra five miles out."

For a moment there was no response, and he was afraid no one was monitoring the radio. He was about to call again, when the welcome answer echoed in the cockpit.

"Roger, George Sierra. We'll be watching for you."

It had been a great experience. Except for the goof just before he reached Nogales, he had flown the task like a contest veteran. He had learned a lot, too, including the fact that you don't make hard-and-fast rules for yourself. Instead you changed your strategy to match the day and the changing conditions.

No other Class B ships had called in for a finish, and Grant had heard only three glass birds crossing the line. He could make out the hangars at the airport and the bone pile of ancient C-47's to one side. He was boring right toward the finish gate, his speed up to 95 knots as he saw he had the field made with altitude to spare.

His radio crackled. It was the gate calling him. "George Sierra, we have you in sight." A moment later, as he eased back on the stick and started a long, breathtaking wing-over, the gate called, "Good Finish, George Sierra. The wind is from the southwest, about five knots on the surface."

"Roger, thank you," Grant said. He rolled out one thousand feet over the field and eased down the flaps to get to proper altitude for pattern entry. There was no traffic at the moment, and he entered downwind at eight hundred feet, turned base at six hundred, and went on to final at a precise four hundred feet. He settled toward the dirt strip short of the runway, touching down lightly and rolling out with a bit of brake right up to the headquarters tent.

Billy Tabor was probably just turning off the Nogales Highway, but other eager helpers caught his wing tip before it could touch down, and then someone was lifting the canopy. Hands reached down in congratulation, and others slapped him on the back.

"Man, what have you got here? A rocket ship?" someone demanded in amazement.

"How did I do?" Grant asked, loosening his harness and pulling himself wearily out of the cockpit.

"No question about Class B if you got your turn-point photos," the contest director told him. "You may even beat a couple of the superships."

"I left pretty early," Grant protested modestly. "They'll be finishing in less elapsed time." But he was elated to know that he had apparently won in his class.

Half a dozen people clustered around, as he walked toward the tent with his roll of film, slapping him on the back and asking about the flight.

"It was a nice little day," he said happily. "I got high and stayed high—except once."

"Good show," somebody said. "You're coming on like gang busters, Grant."

At the tent he checked the takeoff times of the other class B sailplanes. He had been first off, with the latest starter going through the gate twenty-five minutes afterward. It had been ten minutes since he had zapped past the finish line, and no one else had called in except another fiberglass ship and two of the Class C ships completing their shorter task of about 120 miles.

Fifteen minutes later no other Class B contender had yet called the gate, and Grant knew he had made it.

Eager as he was to get a ride to the other side of the field so he could phone his mother and tell her the good news, he decided he had better wait for Billy. Crews needed to be treated with tender loving care, and Billy had done him a big favor on such short notice. So Grant found some shade and watched a gleaming white cirrus make its pull-up after a pass through the gate at red-line speed. Water streamed from the ballast tanks like contrails from a jet to mark the curving path of the hurtling sailplane. It was a beautiful sight as the sun glinted off the vapor.

"Hi, Grant. You had a great day." The voice was vaguely familiar, but Grant wasn't prepared for the shock of seeing Joe Reese when he dropped the hand shading his eyes. The tall man was appreciatively patting the smooth wing of the BG as he walked toward Grant. The smile on his face seemed genuine, and automatically Grant raised his right hand as Reese offered his. Then all his troubles came piling back, and Grant dropped his hand. His face tight, he unloaded on the man.

"Up to now it's been a pretty good day," he said. "What do you want?"

"Hey," Reese protested, his face going sober. "For a contest winner you're mighty edgy. What's the problem?"

"You've got to be kidding," Grant said, keeping his voice low. "Don't you know what your two apes pulled yesterday? I'll be lucky if I don't get busted!"

"You've got me all wrong, Grant," Reese protested, shaking his head firmly. "This is the first I've heard. I was sure I'd talked some sense into them." He was either the greatest con man in the world, or he was telling it straight. No ordinary guy could deadpan like that if he was part of the plot.

"Look," Reese said suddenly, glancing quickly around at the people nearby. "This is a poor place to talk. Come on, I'll buy you a Coke."

Grant nodded his head in grudging agreement and yelled at one of the club members to tell Billy Tabor where he was if he didn't get back before the truck and trailer pulled in. Then he walked quickly with Reese to the other's car and slid into the right-hand seat. As they drove, Grant poured it all out, trying to read Reese's face as he listened to the story of the packet of drugs hidden in the BG. But the surprise seemed genuine, and the apology sounded sincere.

They got out of the car and went inside the coffee shop, finding a table by a window out of earshot of the counter. Reese asked for two Cokes and two hamburgers, and Grant realized suddenly that he was starved.

"Thanks," he said stiffly. "I'll pay for mine."

"I'm sorry you're in a spot, Grant," Reese told him in a low voice. "Those guys *are* crazy, I guess. They have me in a bind too."

"That bit with the ID card," Grant broke in suddenly. "I figured you were telling me you weren't on their side. Why don't you—"

"It's not that easy," Reese said, breaking off as the girl brought their order. When she was back in the kitchen, he went on. "The way it stands, if we try to blow the whistle on them now, you're in hot water. Anyway, I'm gunning for bigger fish and not just these two clowns."

"You *are* a cop then," Grant said with relief.

"Keep it down," Reese said, glancing toward the waitress, who was filling sugar bowls across the room. But she made no sign that she was listening.

"Let's just say that you stumbled onto a messy business, Grant," the man went on. "I'm involved in it myself, and I have to walk a tightrope. Even if I could get you clear of the mess—and I can't right now—I'd still hope you'd hang on a bit longer, so we can wrap the whole thing up. As it is, I'm afraid we have no choice but to play along with whatever they say for a while."

"You mean there'll be more?" Grant demanded.

"With luck, just one more delivery," Reese said, nodding. "Unless we get awfully lucky before that. And I've never been a very lucky guy, I should warn you."

"No dice," Grant said hotly. "They sucked me in once, but I'm sure not going to run dope knowing about it in advance."

"You may have to," Reese told him bluntly. "There's an old saying. 'Might as well hang for a sheep as a lamb.' They've got you cold right now."

"You mean I can only hang once?" Grant said. "Thanks a million."

"It's not all that bad," Reese said, his face softening. "Look, Grant, I have to give these two gorillas credit. They're smart. This thing is working just like they figured it would. You won't get caught; I promise you that. Maybe you'll even get a commendation out of it."

"Just keep me out of prison," Grant said with feeling. "Look, I want to call my mother and let her know about the contest. Then if you'll give me a ride back. . . ."

Reese agreed, but as it turned out, Billy Tabor was just pulling off the highway as Grant finished his call. Joe Reese waved and drove off, leaving Grant to pile into the truck and go back for his sailplane with Billy. Grant told Billy all about the big day and tried to forget the rotten business he had discussed with Reese.

By six o'clock all the contestants were back at the field or had called in from landings out in the boondocks. Everyone was safe, and Grant was in the top slot on the big blackboard for Class B. He had even beaten two of the Class A ships flying the same course!

Billy Tabor was ecstatic, bathing himself in the reflected glory of Grant's victory. "We're going to win that trophy!" he said optimistically. "I can feel it in my bones."

"Great," Grant told him, smiling happily himself. "But we'd better rustle our bones and put the BG in the box, or neither one of us will get home in time for supper."

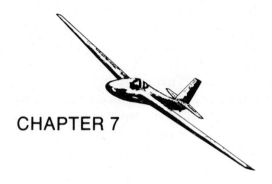

CHAPTER 7

Work at the airport went on. At least Grant was doing something he was interested in, and someday life would smooth out, with a rest once in a while and a chance to do something besides work all the time. As it did on rare occasions, the bitter thought came that the father he had never known was to blame for it all. If Mike Stone had stuck with his airport, life could have been a lot different. Grant often wondered what it would be like to have a father. Sure, some were no bargain, he knew from listening to friends, but it would have been good to have a father he could respect and admire and do things with. And share the BG with.

His mother was great—the greatest, he corrected himself. She was the main reason Grant had stuck it out the way he had. Except for her he'd have been in the Air Force before now. But he owed her too much, he loved her too much, to desert. Besides, they were just breaking even financially. Paying a replacement for him could wipe his mother out.

He was tired when he went in to dinner Monday night. Chopping weeds was a hateful job, and he had done several hours of that around the hangar and along the taxiway. In addition, he had done all the other routine work—two trips into town, three half-hour lessons, and a couple of hours helping Harry tear down the Citabria for its first annual inspection.

However, his mother managed to brighten the evening with a clipping from the local paper describing the sailplane contest. "Area Youth Among Sailplane Winners," the headline said, and he couldn't help smiling as he read it. The write-up was well done, and it mentioned Grant as "winning the Class B event decisively, in spite of the fact that this was his first competition flight."

"How does it feel to be famous?" his mother asked, propping her chin on both hands and smiling at him proudly.

"On page fourteen I'm famous?" he responded. But he was still smiling, a little self-consciously but enjoying the idea of being in the news. The thought came that he would be asked to describe his win at the pilots' meeting before the next contest on Sunday. As a public speaker Grant had won no prizes, and he knew he'd have more butterflies in that role than he did flying the 235 miles.

"I'm so proud of my son, the soaring pilot," his mother told him. "You were born to fly, Grant. I'm sure you know that."

"Well, I don't actively dislike the sport," he admitted with a grin as he put the clipping down. "It beats working."

"That's another thing," his mother added. "You're the hardest worker I know. Even Harry says he's never seen anybody as dependable as you."

"He's just buttering up the boss," Grant said, helping himself to more chili. "You knew we tore down the Citabria today?"

"Right. I've scratched it for the week. If we get in a bind, we can borrow another 150 from the Donahues."

"Too bad we can't *buy* another one," Grant said, frowning.

"If wishes were horses, beggars would ride," his mother quoted.

"Penny-wise, pound-foolish," he responded. "We're losing a lot of flight-instruction business, Mom."

"Mr. Jones says maybe in the spring we can afford another plane," his mother said. "We'll manage till then."

"Mr. Jones," Grant repeated with a snort. "He's never even been *in* a plane! Look, suppose we had a sudden five thousand dollars—"

"Oh, no!" she said, shaking her head. "We don't rob banks, even to purchase much-needed equipment."

"I think I might get that much for the BG," Grant said slowly, poking at his food.

"The BG?" his mother cried. "Don't be silly, Grant. You're going to be *flying* the BG for years. Unless you move up to something better, that is."

"I don't know," he said tightly. "Everything went sour when I started flying the sailplane."

"That was just a freak coincidence," his mother said, reaching over to touch his arm. "It could have happened to anyone."

"Sure, any nut flying a sailplane. If I got rid of it, they couldn't ask me to—"

"To what, dear?" His mother's face was worried now, and she kept her hand on his.

"To smuggle dope," he said angrily. "I might as well tell you all of it." And he did, while she listened in horror.

"Oh, no, Grant," she said in a whisper. "I'm so sorry. I knew I should have done something."

"What could you do?" he asked, almost angrily. "We don't know how to deal with snakes like that. I should have *made* you leave the state."

"I'm sorry," she repeated. "I'm so sorry. I guess I just couldn't believe it was happening. You hear about this terrible dope business all the time, but you can't believe

87

you'll be mixed up in it. Thank the Lord you're not involved in another way, Grant."

"Don't worry," he told her firmly. "I've seen too many other guys hooked on the stuff. But I'm still in big trouble, Mom."

"Now we *are* going to the sheriff," she said decisively. "We must stop these dangerous men."

"This guy Reese," Grant broke in. "He's my one hope. He's cagey about it, but I think he's working with the narcs and trying to set these two apes up for a bust."

"Narcs?" she repeated, wrinkling her forehead.

"Narcotics agents," he explained. "Mom, Reese was at Ryan Field after the contest. The guy is everywhere. He must know when I go to the bathroom even. He says if I'll give it one more shot, those guys can be nailed, and I'll be in the clear."

"But maybe you won't be," his mother protested. "Why can't we call the sheriff right now?"

"Because our phone could be bugged," he told her. "Maybe somebody's watching the house. Mom, I don't want anything to happen to you!"

"Neither do I," she admitted. "But before I'll put you in danger, I'll risk that to bring the police in."

"Right now the police might throw *me* in jail," he reminded her. "Those two gorillas have pictures of drugs coming out of the BG. And they can probably prove I made that flight out of Mexico with it in the sailplane."

"What are we going to do then?" his mother asked in despair.

"I'm going to have a piece of pie," he said. "Maybe it will help me think."

They had settled nothing with the long discussion, but in the end his mother agreed to rock along for a few days before calling the authorities. Much as she detested the drug traffic, she was hesitant to endanger Grant's life. So was

Grant. There seemed to be no other course but to plunge back into the business of running the airport and to try to keep their minds off the heavy shadow hanging over them.

It happened on Saturday. Grant had caught up on his work temporarily and was taking a few minutes to check over the BG for the contest the next day. Harry had scrounged a twenty-two-cubic-foot oxygen tank for him, and Grant had borrowed a regulator and mask from their 182. He was in the BG's cockpit, mounting brackets for the tank when someone said, "Hello." He looked over his shoulder and found himself staring at one of the bearded smugglers. Anger at the man's nerve mixed with Grant's fear of trouble.

"Don't put too much garbage back there," the doper said, nodding toward the compartment. "We've got another delivery set up for you for tomorrow, and this one will be a little larger than that trial run we did the other day."

"You're crazy," Grant told him. "Now get out of here, or I go to the cops. Understand?"

"Look, kid, don't get hard with me," the man said, and the amused smile vanished. "Since you insisted on nosing around, we decided to let you make yourself useful."

"I said No," Grant told him again.

"Wait till you hear it all. We blew a job last month for the big man."

"Big man?"

"We're just mules, kid. We work on commission. But last time the narcs busted our pilot, and we barely saved our skins. This time it's got to go. Understand?"

"No," Grant said.

"The narcs are hot on airplanes lately," the man said impatiently. "So we don't use one. We buy from a guy across the border. You deliver to our field, and Reese gets it to the big man. And he pays us instead of breaking our heads."

With a sick feeling Grant remembered the time the man had shoved a gun in his stomach, but he had had it with the whole stupid business.

"Harry!" he yelled suddenly to the mechanic working on the Citabria in the back corner of the hangar. "I need you. And bring a big wrench!"

Watching the beefy redhead step down from his workstand and come their way, wrench in hand, the doper backed off. Then he shrugged and said, "Okay, wise guy, we'll be in touch. We'll see whether you go or not!" He moved out of the hangar fast, with Harry on his heels.

Grant listened with relief as car tires screeched on gravel, but he was still shaking when Harry came back, wiping his hands on a rag.

"What did Godzilla want?" the mechanic demanded.

"For me to run dope for them," Grant said hotly.

"Arrogant jerk!" Harry exploded. "I should have creamed him when I had the chance."

"Just as well you didn't. He probably had a gun, and he would have used it."

A sudden fear hit Grant then, and he yelled as the mechanic walked back to the Citabria. "Harry, where's Mom?"

"She went into town to see old man Jones," Harry said. "Said she'd be back in time for supper."

Oh, no! Grant thought, climbing stiffly out of the sailplane. No wonder the smuggler was so cocky. Quickly he ran over to the pickup and got on the highway toward town, pushing the old truck as hard as it would go. His mother wasn't at the accountant's office. He had been afraid she wouldn't be. But just as he was about to panic, he spotted her car and managed to flag her down. She

90

was fine, and had seen nothing that would indicate she was in danger. Only reluctantly did she leave the car at a filling station to ride back with Grant.

It was strange the way things worked out. There was a man waiting in the office for them when they got back to the hangar. At first Grant thought he was interested in flight training and was all set to give him the sales pitch. But the man shook his head and took out a wallet. He showed them a card identifying him as an investigator in the Department of Public Safety. A warning bell rang in Grant's head and he frowned.

"I've seen other badges lately," he said. "How do we know you really are this guy?"

"Call the office in Phoenix and ask for a description of me," the man said evenly. "Here's the number. You can verify it in your phone book."

"It's all right, Grant," his mother said softly. Then she told the man, "Won't you sit down?"

"Thank you, ma'am," the man said, replacing his wallet and sitting down. "I'm checking out leads on dope smuggling, and I just learned that you had a glider stolen. Is that right?"

"That's right," Grant said, on guard at once. "We reported it to the sheriff."

"And he recovered it for you?"

"Uh . . . no," Grant said. "I found the sailplane. And the trailer was brought back. A . . . kind of misunderstanding, I guess."

"You want to tell me about it?" the agent asked.

"Grant," his mother said urgently. "Let's tell him the whole story. Please?"

For a moment Grant was going to refuse. Then he gave up. "Okay, Mom," he said, more relieved than he could

91

believe. Something told him this man already knew a lot. "If he can promise that you'll be safe, I'll tell him the whole bit."

"I'll do my best," the agent said. "Let's have it."

Ten minutes later he had all the details and had written down a page of notes.

"Can't you arrest these smugglers right now?" Grant's mother asked eagerly.

"No, ma'am," the agent said. "In the first place, I'd have a hard time finding them. Second, who can prove anything at this point? It would be your word against theirs. I have an idea who the two rough-looking dopers are. Reese I'm not familiar with, except I'm sure that's not his name."

"Great," Grant said disappointedly. "You mean we're right back where we started?"

"No," the man said. "I'll have four men working for you shortly. They may not be the best mechanics in the world, but nobody will give you any trouble as long as they're here. And I've got a question for you. Are you willing to go through with the deal the dopers have set you up for?"

"No, Grant!" his mother cried. "It's too dangerous even to consider."

"Just a minute, ma'am," the investigator told her patiently. "If he turns these apes down, we don't know what they might do. And I can't keep a guard here indefinitely. Okay? Now, if Grant flies this trip, they won't touch him until he lands with the stuff. And we can arrange it so that by then we have these dopers under arrest."

"They're pretty shrewd types," Grant said. "And hard as they come."

"No argument," the man said. "I've known their kind for eight years. But we're dealing with just three men, and we've got a lot more troops than that. We also have some equipment that will come in handy. Well?"

"Should we do it, Grant?" his mother asked hesitantly. "If we're sure you'll be safe—"

"Okay," Grant said. "Anything is better than what we've been going through. What do we do now?"

It was basically a simple plan that the investigator sketched. Four agents would look out for Mrs. Stone. Others would infiltrate the secret strip where Grant was to land with the narcotics. If something went wrong, they could warn him by radio, and he could divert and land somewhere else for safety. Finally, Harry Shaughnessy would crew for Grant in the contest.

It might work, Grant had to agree. Nothing he could think of seemed to have a better chance of success.

"Now that we have that settled," the investigator said with a grin, "how about my familiarization ride in one of your aircraft? I learned to fly a long time ago, but I think I can fake it, just in case any of our friends are keeping an eye on us."

The Narcotics Division "troops" began arriving soon after the investigator left. Grant and his mother had clued Harry in on the plan by then, and the first thing the suspicious mechanic did was to pick up the phone and ask the operator for the Department of Public Safety office in Phoenix. Blunt as the back of an ax, he got right to the point.

"This is Harry Shaughnessy at Stone Airport," he said when the call went through. "A man claiming to be on your investigation staff was here. Could you verify his visit, and give me his physical description, please?"

After the call was completed, Harry nodded his satisfaction. "I'll buy the guy," he said. He turned to the agents. "Okay, you people, you'll find coveralls in the locker over there. And there are a couple of cots back in that corner.

93

Mrs. Stone will coach you in the morning, so you can make like mechanics."

"Thanks," one of the men said with a smile. "But cots won't get much use, I'm afraid."

After Harry left, Grant suddenly remembered that he hadn't completed the oxygen hookup in his BG. At first he shrugged, wondering what difference it made now and why the thought had come to him so strongly. Then he decided to go out to the hangar and complete the job anyhow. Maybe someday, when things were sane again, he could make use of the oxygen. To get his Diamond Altitude badge, he would have to climb nearly 17,000 feet above his release point, and he couldn't hold his breath that high. And the work would give him something to do until he got groggy enough to go to sleep.

The four agents had vanished already, and it was weirdly lonesome in the big hangar as he worked. Outside a warm wind sighed faintly, and once in a while he caught the whine of a jet high overhead. But the hangar itself was like a metal tomb. The light was poor too, so that by the time he tightened the last fitting, he had a ringing headache and was glad to call it quits. He latched the canopy in place, covered it carefully, and then rolled the fuselage back into the trailer.

The air was warm as he walked to the house, but so clear that the stars popped out of the dark bowl of the sky. It should be another good day for a contest.

"Who's there?" someone asked from the shadows as he reached the porch.

"Grant Stone," he said, blinking in the beam of a flash-light.

"Just checking," an agent told him. "Good night."

"Good night," Grant said. "And thanks." He really meant it.

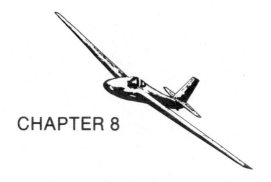

CHAPTER 8

Despite the fat man's threat, none of the three smugglers had been in touch with Grant about the proposed flight. Grant halfheartedly hoped he would not hear from them, and that he might be off the hook. But it was a vain hope. Reese was there at the airport waiting for him on the day of the contest.

"Good luck, champ," he said, and when he shook hands, he left a folded paper in Grant's hand. "Just one more time should do it." And then the tall man was gone, so fast that Harry had not even been aware of the contact.

"Son of a gun!" he said in disappointment. "Too bad one of our friends wasn't here to grab him."

"They may be here," Grant said, looking around carefully. "But there'd be no point in nailing Reese till we get the goods on him."

"You're right. So what's the plan he passed you?"

Feeling guilty and conspicuous, Grant unfolded the paper, which turned out to be a piece of an aeronautical chart with the Mexican pickup point circled in green. It was well chosen. From it Reese had drawn a line ending at the strip north of the border that had involved Grant in the affair. Some radio frequencies were also listed, and there was a tentative timetable.

"Looks like you've got your work cut out for you," Harry said soberly.

"So we'll get it over with," Grant said. "I guess . . ."

He broke off as someone shouted his name from the contest headquarters tent. In all the excitement, he had forgotten he would be asked to describe his winning flight of the week before, and when the contest director called on him, he stuttered and stammered a little before he got going. Then he briefly described his flight.

"Beginner's luck," he told them. "It was a fantastic day, as you all know. Except for just before that second turn point, where I got overconfident, there was no sweat. Oh, yeah, I didn't have any oxygen, so I had to stay pretty low. Today I have oxygen."

Groans from other Class B entrants mixed with a spatter of applause as he sat down. It *was* a good showing for a beginner, and he earnestly wished he could try for a repeat today. He barely heard the report of the Class A winner, who had blasted around the long triangle at seventy-three miles an hour.

Billy Tabor showed up, expecting to crew for him again, and Grant found it a little sticky explaining about Harry and getting across the idea that Billy couldn't go along. It was going to be hard enough to duck out of the contest without having someone along who wasn't in on the plan.

"I'm sorry, Billy," Grant told the boy. "But—"

"No problem," Tabor said with a philosophical shrug. "Maybe they can use me at the gate or something. Good luck, champ."

"Thanks," Grant said, feeling like a traitor.

The task for the contest, as Grant—and Joe Reese—had expected, was again mapped out toward the south. The first turn point was the airstrip at Tombstone, and the second was Willcox Airport just north of Willcox Playa, a huge dry lake that often showed up in NASA space photos. The total distance was only 160 miles for both Class A and Class B, since the weather briefing predicted somewhat weaker conditions than they had had the week before.

"It's a shame you can't win this one too," Harry said. "I underrated you glider nuts. I had no idea there was this much interest."

"That's because you keep yourself stuck inside an engine," Grant told him, grinning. "There's more to life than pistons and crankshafts."

"Especially right now," Harry agreed. "You better check me out fast on procedures, so I can behave like a real ground crew."

"No problem," Grant said. "The BG is all set. My take-off time is not till twelve fifty-eight. They reversed the order from last week to even things up."

"But how about hooking up the towline and running your wing and all that?" Harry asked. "We fat boys have problems."

"Somebody on the line will do that," Grant assured him. "All you have to do is follow me with the trailer. Let's check that code we worked out again. We want it to sound legit on the radio."

This time Grant had decided they'd better use code for the check points, including the Mexican strip where he was to make the drug pickup. Working backward with the alphabet, he had assigned the name Zulu to the abandoned Sahuarita strip twenty miles southeast of Ryan Field, Yankee to the dirt strip at Mescal on the Benson Highway, X Ray to Tombstone, and Whiskey to the Mexican strip thirty miles southwest.

"I'll keep you informed," Grant promised. "Play it by ear, and pray a lot. The real task today is to keep Mom safe. Right?"

"Right," Harry said. "We better knock it off. Here comes some kind of an official."

It was the photo man, carrying a card marked with the BG's contest letters GS and the date. Grant put the canopy on, and the official made a grease-pencil mark on the plastic just in front of the camera lens. Then Grant reached through the vent and snapped the shutter, taking an identification picture of the board. To be acceptable, his photos of turn points would have to be on this same roll of film, and include the same blurred smudge from the grease-pencil mark.

"You people don't mess around," Harry said approvingly. "Quite a science."

"We try," Grant said. Contest procedure was carefully worked out to eliminate all the bugs. There was more to a task than just hot flying, and many a contest had been lost because of bad photos or some other technicality. But rules were rules.

The waiting was an agony of tension. Grant was shaken when the early starters found very weak conditions, and several had to land for relights. Even two of the fiberglass sailplanes were unable to stay airborne and had to settle back to the runway. Then the day began to improve, and he heaved a relieved sigh as pilots gained altitude. Ten minutes before his scheduled takeoff, one of the Soaring Club 1-26's called the gate for a start. Cumulus clouds were beginning to form over Mount Lemmon. It would be all right.

"Let's go," he told Harry, and together they pulled the BG on an angle toward the runway. Three minutes later he was buckled in, with the canopy secured, the towline attached, and the control action checked.

The wingman looked at Grant for a ready signal and hoisted the wing. The towplane, a Citabria this time, moved down the runway, taking up rope slack, and then began fanning its rudder. Grant stepped on his rudder pedals in answer, scanned the situation to left and right, and braced himself for his second contest takeoff. This contest would be far different, and his only prize would be his mother's safety. He caught himself clearing his throat nervously as they started to move.

Flying cautiously, he didn't go through the start gate until 1:20. By then the thermals were averaging about 400 feet a minute, and he had no difficulty finding them.

Several miles southeast of the start gate, and climbing smoothly through 7000 feet, he called Harry. "George Sierra Ground, you can move out. And switch to Channel five."

Grant flipped the knob on his own radio to the different frequency. That way, there would be less interference with start-gate communications, and fewer people hearing his calls to Harry. Besides, Joe Reese had specified that Grant use 123.5 as much as he could.

He moved out steadily, retracing almost exactly his route of a week ago. Thermal strength was not the same, however, and he knew his speed wouldn't be as fast today. Not that it made any difference to him as a contestant, but it would take longer to complete the illegal task the smugglers had set for him. Sighting along his right wing at the weed-covered onetime Air Force landing field at Sahuarita, he pressed the mike switch and gave Harry his positions.

"George Sierra, five miles left of Zulu. At eighty-five."

"Roger, George Sierra," came the quick answer. "I'm just getting on the Freeway."

Harry understood effective radio communication. Grant grinned to himself as he thought of the chatter that would be heard on Channel 3. In spite of briefings before the contest, there would be the inevitable and interminable dialogue between harried pilots and nervous ground crews. Carrying on long-winded discussions about what kind of gas to put in the car or what was the matter with the pilot's mike, they would block out some poor soul who was trying to contact the gate for a start. Grant had learned long ago that generally the less you said, the better you communicated. Today that would be especially true.

In spite of the beautiful, cloud-studded blue sky and the smooth swish of the sailplane surrounding him, his body felt tight, and he was churning inside. Adding to his tenseness was a sudden battle with a strong sink about twenty miles south of Point Zulu. He watched his 8500 feet of altitude dwindle to under 5000 before the wind riding up the Whetstones boosted him skyward again. He caught a strong thermal over Apache Peak, his first boomer of the day, and rode it to a comforting 10,500 feet.

"George Sierra, eight miles right of Yankee. Ten-five and cruising."

"Roger, George Sierra. Ground, ten beyond Yankee."

"Push on to X Ray, George Sierra Ground."

Two clicks on the mike answered Grant, and he settled back in the seat. For the first time that day he relaxed a little. It was a temptation to head straight south for the rendezvous across the border, but he controlled the urge. He and Harry had planned that he would make the first turn point and take his picture. Only then would he head south. If something went wrong, he could always say he had trouble and found lift only in that direction.

Slowly the road and railroad that had been far to his left angled toward him. He could see the small crossroads railroad settlement at Fairbank, and beyond it historic Tombstone, tiny from ten thousand feet. The sky was half covered with puffy cumulus clouds now. To his right the lofty Huachuca Mountains were shrouded in a line of them leading to the southern horizon.

He punched the shutter of the camera at 2:29, estimating his average speed for the leg at under 45 miles an hour. There was plenty of lift, but it was weaker than if there had been fewer clouds. The cloud base would probably not go much above 10,500 feet today. He shrugged and searched the sky for other sailplanes. He picked up the white flash of a glass bird far to the north, but there was nothing anywhere near him. Relieved, he broke off his circling over Tombstone and headed southwest instead of toward the second turn at Willcox.

"George Sierra, leaving Point X Ray for Whiskey," he radioed.

The use of the code word brought back his tenseness. Thirty miles ahead was a dirt strip where he would contact someone and pick up a package of heroin. The thought sickened him, but there was no help for that now. He eased the stick forward and headed for the Mule Mountains at 70 knots.

There was a restricted area, marked on his chart, around Fort Huachuca, the big Army Electronic Proving Grounds, but he could skirt that with no trouble. It seemed risky to fly so close to so much radar and other sophisticated gear, but he knew he was comparatively safe from detection. The army was probably used to sailplanes in the area, and in the rare possibility that he was tracked on a radar scope, they would not hit the panic button.

The radio crackled, and Harry reported that he was holding at his designated point. Harry's instructions were to stay near Bisbee until he heard otherwise from Grant.

"Roger, George Sierra Ground. George Sierra is about ten miles short of Point Whiskey. According to plan."

Then, on an impulse, he added, "Wish me luck!" He was going to need a lot.

"Good luck, Grant," Harry said, his voice low and earnest. "Yell if you need me."

Grant clicked his mike button and settled down to the task of making good his rendezvous at Point Whiskey. When Highway 80 branched east to pick up Bisbee, he left it and swung farther to his right, now that he was clear of the Fort Huachuca restricted area. Thompson Airport was in sight, just east of the railroad tracks. He noted its elevation on his map and figured his altitude above the ground to be about four thousand feet. With only fifteen miles to go, he should make his destination with no problem.

Nervously he kept his head swiveling, hoping no one was around to see him cross the border. There were no aircraft in sight, but he still held his breath.

He floated across the east-west highway, his last checkpoint before entering Mexico. Three more miles, just under three minutes. He checked his watch, and moments later he knew he was flying illegally in a foreign country.

But that was the least of his worries. The BG bumped through a patch of fairly strong lift, and Grant had to nose down to keep from climbing. He wanted to keep his approach as unobtrusive as possible. In soft shadow under an almost solid cloud deck, the BG should not be too easy to see, especially if he made no sudden maneuvers.

His heart seemed to hammer as he caught sight of the small town ahead of him, with a narrow dirt strip beyond it. This must be his destination, the rendezvous they had coded Whiskey. Almost as he spotted it, the radio crackled.

"George Sierra," he heard in surprise. "Have you in sight." And then he knew it must be the smugglers. They weren't missing a bet. A casual listener would have taken the voice for his ground crew.

"George Sierra, at Point Whiskey," he responded. That would keep Harry posted.

A thousand feet over the dirt strip, he rolled into his downwind leg and eased back on the flap handle, at the same time matching the ballooning tendency of the sailplane by pushing the stick forward. The BG floated down at a steep angle as he banked into his base leg and made his final turn. Tensely he studied the terrain.

Then he was on the ground, working the stick to hold his wings level as he killed off forward speed with the brake. By the time he had stopped, a man was trotting from the brush toward him. It was the fat one.

Grant had expected them to be far more cautious. He was sure he would be put to some kind of test or made to wait a long time. But slowly he realized that it would have been difficult for anyone to have duplicated his BG, the license and contest numbers, the radio code, and the rest. They probably wouldn't even frisk him, because *he* was the one on the spot, with his mother's safety held over his head until the successful completion of the affair.

"Very nice," the man called as he approached the nose. "Ready for your air freight, kid?"

Grant nodded silently, his feelings a mixture of anger, frustration, and fear. The man was carrying a small flight bag, and Grant's mouth dropped open in surprise. He had expected a small package, like the one they had hidden in his sailplane, but this was apparently a wholesale order.

As he took off the canopy, he protested. "That much weight could put me out of balance," he said, shaking his head. But the man laughed at him as he set to work removing the seat back and panel.

"Don't put me on!" the man said. "This whole thing is less than ten pounds, and it will all be at your center of gravity. Now listen good. I'm putting this bag on your wheel doors. If you are positive there's no other way out, drop your landing gear and that will get rid of the evidence. But it better be life or death, because if you show up at our field without this stuff, a couple of people may end up dead. Understand?"

"Thanks a lot," Grant said tightly.

"Don't take it too hard, kid. Keep your nose clean and everybody wins. Your old lady doesn't get hurt, and you can get back to your fun and games. After this deal we won't have to bother you anymore. We won't have to bother *anybody!* You got any idea how much three kilos of horse is worth?"

"No," Grant said.

"Too bad you don't have a piece of this action," the man said. "You'll be carrying close to half a million bucks for the big man. So you better not goof. Understand?"

"I understand," Grant said. "Be careful of my control wires down there."

"I know what I'm doing," the man assured him from his crouching position as he put the panel back. "Now get back in this thing, and I'll hook you up. How fast do you want to be towed? And how high?"

"Sixty-five miles an hour," Grant said. "I don't know how high . . . two thousand feet if I'm lucky."

"Get real lucky. Okay? And make it to our strip as quick as you can. You ought to know where it is by now."

"I know exactly where it is," Grant said, nodding. "Is your pilot checked out on towing?"

"Kid, we're checked out on *everything*," the man told him with a grin. "I'll even run your wing for you. Okay?"

"Okay," Grant said. A plane taxied from behind some

104

trees, and he caught the sound of the engine. The man quickly replaced the canopy over him and then took out his handkerchief and dusted it lightly. Grant latched it and snugged his harness straps, and while he waited, he began to sweat in the ovenlike heat.

Kneeling in the dirt, the man outside hooked the tow ring onto the BG's release hook and made an okay sign to Grant. As the plane got into position and the man moved quickly toward it, Grant had the crazy feeling he was still flying in the contest.

There was a slightly quartering headwind, and the take-off was uneventful. Grant felt the bump of a strong thermal at twelve hundred feet above the ground and almost released. But he thought better of it and hung on until the plane towing him had made a slow 360-degree turn. He blundered into the lift again at just over two thousand feet, and the variometer needle responded immediately. Its audio signal shrilled in Grant's ears as he pulled the release. He was on his own now, and he wondered how the dopers would react to the change in plans dreamed up for them.

Glancing at his watch, he noted with satisfaction that it had been only about twelve minutes since he had touched down on the strip. The faster he got back across the border, the better he would feel. Clipping his mike onto his collar, he squeezed the button atop the stick and called Harry.

"George Sierra got low over Point Whiskey. Now have strong lift and will be proceeding to Point Victor." To his relief, it was Harry who answered. There was no mistaking the loud-voiced Irishman.

"Roger, George Sierra. Proceeding to Victor." That was all, but it was enough.

Grant settled down to the serious business of gaining altitude under the line of clouds so that he could work his way to the northwest and Point Victor. He prayed that the coincidence of code names was a good omen, and a thrill of satisfaction ran through him as he thought how the smugglers would take it when they found out what was happening.

He crossed the highway again, climbing through eight thousand feet and flying straight on course under the line of heavy clouds. He was relieved to be back in his own country again, even with the load of narcotics behind him.

It was nearly four o'clock when the radio crackled again. This time he stiffened in surprise. It was his mother's voice.

"George Sierra, this is Cessna Four-Three-Two-Two-Charley. Over." That was their plane.

"George Sierra," he fired back. "Mom, what are you doing in—"

"I'm sorry, Grant," came the answer. "I have to tell you to change your destination. Fly direct to Picnic Valley. Repeat, Picnic Valley. Understood?"

"Two-Two-Charley, I do *not* understand. Please clarify."

"No problem," a masculine voice said. "Proceed to Picnic Valley, George Sierra. We will both meet you there. Acknowledge." And that was Joe Reese!

Still holding his heading for the original destination they had coded Victor, Grant quickly comprehended the situation. Somehow, in spite of all the narcotics people's efforts, his mother had been kidnapped. Now she was in their Cessna with Joe Reese, and urging Grant to abandon the original plan and fly to Picnic Valley, a tiny rough strip they had found long ago to the north of Stone Field and used for an occasional picnic lunch. What was Reese up to?

"Acknowledge, George Sierra," Reese repeated, his voice tighter. "And keep your answer brief. Or I can't be responsible for keeping the bargain."

"Two-Two-Charley, George Sierra understands," Grant

said desperately, knowing he had no choice. "Proceeding to Picnic Valley."

He swung the nose to the right on a new heading, praying that Harry had heard and understood what was happening. Grant had caught the warning in Reese's last message, and he was afraid to try to alert Harry or the narcs either. Sure, the agents would be monitoring the frequency, but they would have no idea where Picnic Valley was. The name was one Grant himself had thought up when he was much younger. Only he, his mother, and Harry knew its location by that name.

He had no idea if they were tracking him visually. He doubted it very much. Spotting a high-flying sailplane from the ground was next to impossible, and likely the narcs wouldn't have a plane in the area for fear of scaring off the dopers.

For several seconds Grant was afraid he would hear Harry's big voice acknowledging that he was en route to Picnic Valley, but there was no call. Either the mechanic had not heard the air-to-air transmission, or he was playing it smart and keeping his mouth shut. Grant hoped it was the latter case, and that Harry was barreling the truck and trailer north toward the new rendezvous. He had a gun with him, and he and Grant should be a match for Reese in ensuring his mother's safety.

He wondered how they had managed to trap his mother, and why there had been the sudden switch in plans. Had all three smugglers gotten wind of the trap the agents were setting up at the original site? Or was this Reese's doing because he was working with the authorities as an informer?

Grant was still trying vainly to unscramble the puzzle when something shot past him just over his canopy and froze his hand on the stick. The Cessna 150 that had towed him from the Mexican strip half an hour ago was now turning steeply and heading back toward him on a collision course! The guy wasn't kidding!

Grant realized he had goofed badly, as he evaded the Cessna's second pass by rolling inverted and doing a split-S out the bottom as the Cessna passed overhead. The plane must have been following him all the way to make sure he went where he was supposed to. Now the crazy pilot was trying to knock him out of the sky in this deserted area, figuring he could retrieve the drugs from the wrecked glider. Grant had been afraid before for his mother. Now he was fighting for his own life.

He brought the BG level, five hundred feet below the altitude where the plane had buzzed him. At this rate he was going to be forced onto the ground in a hurry.

There was one whisper of a chance—to find a strong thermal and outclimb the attacking plane. Desperately he prayed for lift, and as the plane closed the distance between them, the variometer squealed. He racked the BG into a tight bank to the right, and climbing at better than 500 feet a minute, worked desperately to center the thermal and increase that rate.

His good fortune had thwarted his pursuer momentarily, and he next caught sight of the 150 well below him as it banked around for another pass. It came after him in a shallow climbing turn, its motor winding up loudly.

The BG was climbing now in the strong thermal at 800 feet a minute, and for the moment Grant kept out of reach. But then a sudden realization chilled him. The base of the cloud was probably only about three thousand feet above him. He was going to be squeezed into a trap! Unable to work the lift with him, the pilot of the heavier, less-maneuverable power plane would nevertheless catch him when he could no longer climb. And the pilot was evidently ready to risk a collision, hoping to damage the sailplane and send it plunging to earth. But there was nothing else to do except continue to climb as fast as he could.

All too soon he contacted the wisps of vapor that streamed out of the base of the cloud. For a frightening moment he lost the thermal and lift turned to sink, but he was able to snake around and find something going up again before the 150 caught him. He heard its engine rise in a fury of sound and fade out as it passed below him. Then he was *in* the cloud and had lost sight of the ground far below.

There was no artificial horizon on the panel of the BG. The instrument was not legal in a contest, and Grant hadn't had the money for one anyhow. He did have the yaw string and the compass, though, not to mention all the hours he had flown on instruments. Gingerly he centered the controls and carefully watched the airspeed. The lift was strong, and not yet too turbulent. Keeping the compass on 290 degrees, he let the ship fly itself laterally while he concentrated on the rudder to hold the heading. He had learned that trick a long time ago. When you were flying blind, it was nearly impossible to manage all the controls, but the ship's natural stability would keep it level unless the air got too rough.

Cloud flying was illegal. Worse yet, it was dangerous. Grant knew of cases where power planes, and sailplanes too, had come diving out of the bottom of a cloud in steep spirals and the wings had been pulled off before control was regained. And in a cloud you could run into somebody else—including a crazed 150 pilot, who saw half a million dollars worth of heroin slipping out of his grasp.

But Grant had no alternative that he could think of, so he hung in there. His ears strained for any sound of the plane's engine. All he heard were the swish of the BG's wings through the gray murk and the hiss of air around the canopy. He could see nothing beyond that canopy but the yaw string, streaming now with condensation, but that was all right, because his attention was centered on the instruments.

The compass heading held, and the variometer continued to whistle its signal. The altimeter had passed thirteen thousand feet before Grant remembered that he had oxygen. He reached awkwardly for the mask behind him, and then sucked eagerly on the rich stuff. All he needed in this spot was to pass out from lack of air; if he did, he'd go shooting out the bottom of the cloud like a rocket.

Still climbing better than 500 feet a minute and passing fifteen thousand feet, the BG suddenly began to lurch like a rubber raft in the rapids. Clamping his jaws, Grant fought for control. He watched the airspeed like a hawk and gently moved the stick when he seemed to be rolling. Then, just when he thought he was losing control, the bucking smoothed, and the fog melted away. The BG slid out of the side of the huge cloud into crystal-smooth lift of about 200 feet a minute.

He had heard of the phenomenon. It was a "wave" lift rising over a massive line of cumulus clouds instead of a mountain. He rode it unbelievingly, grateful for the oxygen mask as the altimeter climbed toward sixteen thousand feet. Nowhere was there a sign of the pursuing power plane, and Grant began to hope that he had rid himself of that problem.

Safe for a moment, he forced himself to relax and plan his next move, which was to reach the new rendezvous Reese had spelled out, the isolated valley between two low ranges ten miles north of Stone Field.

Orienting himself quickly, Grant picked out Keystone Peak some ten miles away in the desert, and lined up on that. Then, with his heading established, he got out his glide computer and calculated a maximum speed that would get him to the valley without further climbing. He would get there ten minutes earlier than the estimate he had made earlier—thanks to his frightening elevator ride inside the churning cumulus cloud. He called Reese and gave him the new estimated arrival time.

On the horizon he thought he could make out the low range that hid his destination. Grimly he wondered what he would find when he reached it with his cargo.

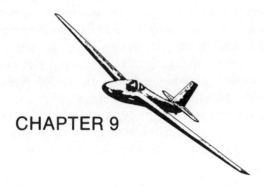

CHAPTER 9

Grant had expected Reese to be there waiting, so it was no surprise to see the Cessna standing near the north end of the short landing strip. His main worry was whether or not his mother was still in the plane, and unharmed.

In spite of the tension building in him, Grant forced himself to glance at the checklist on the panel to his left: airspeed, landing gear, flaps. His pattern speed was right on the nose, and he reached for the gear handle. It stuck. He yanked at it, but it still did not budge. Desperately he yanked again, and it finally moved, maybe a quarter of an inch.

With a shout of frustration, Grant eased on the flaps and started his turn. Then, letting the flap handle go for a second, he yanked one last time at the gear. Nothing happened, and he knew suddenly that the small flight bag of drugs had come loose from its place on the wheel doors and was fouling up the bell crank that actuated the gear. Because of it, he would soon be making his first wheel-up landing.

Back on the flaps now, his teeth clamped together angrily, Grant angled the BG down as steeply as he dared. Releasing the flaps to try one more yank on the gear had caused the sailplane to balloon high as he approached the strip and now the Cessna ahead of him was far too close.

With the brake it would have been no problem. Grant could have put the BG up on its nose and ground to a quick stop. But he had no brakes at all now, and the sailplane touched down gently on the brushing soil with hardly any tendency to slow.

Through the plexiglass canopy he saw the Cessna increase in size as if someone were pumping it up, and he watched paralyzed as two people—one of them his mother —began frantically to push the airplane out of the way. It was too little and too late.

For part of a second Grant thought of continuing his uncontrolled slide right into the power plane. That would put it out of commission and maybe result in Reese's capture. But at the last minute he shook his head, knowing he might hurt his mother in such a collision. Desperately he shoved the stick to the left, bunching his muscles against the impact.

The left wing slashed at the ground, its tip catching on the mesquite, as he had hoped it would. After that he was only vaguely aware of what was happening. Mainly he was aware of noise, the noise of his beautiful bird breaking up in a vicious ground loop. Somehow he seemed to be taking off again, and then he saw the brush-covered ground coming straight at him. The nose structure crumpled on impact, and his knees jammed up into his chest. There was more smashing as the right wing contacted the ground, and a blur of color as the Cessna crossed his line of vision. Then it was quiet.

Somehow he had the canopy off and was trying to unfasten the straps and chute harness when he heard his mother's cry. Then they were both there, one on each side of him, his mother holding him and crying all over him, while Joe Reese carefully ran his hand down Grant's still doubled-up legs.

"Do they hurt?" the tall man asked, real concern in his face.

"I have felt better," Grant managed to say. "If you could just help me get out. . . ."

When he was sure no bones were broken, Reese lifted Grant out of the smashed cockpit and sat him down on the ground. Still crying, Grant's mother softly rubbed his bleeding shins while Grant gritted his teeth.

"I'm okay," he managed at last. His head had cleared quickly, and it seemed that except for the skin he had lost scraping his legs under the instrument panel, he was in one piece. "Are *you* all right?" he demanded of his mother as he pushed himself to his feet.

"Yes, now I am," she said. "I'm so relieved it's nearly over."

"Now to get this evidence into the plane," Reese said, a broad smile on his face as he bent to the box Grant had removed from the sailplane. "We've got the goods on those two clowns, Grant, and—"

"Oh, stop it!" Grant's mother cried suddenly. "Don't lie to him, Mike. I can't stand any more of this sick farce."

Grant whirled in amazement, shocked at the twisted look of anger and disgust on his mother's face as she glared at Reese.

"Mom," he said softly. "What—"

"Grant," she said, obviously fighting to control her voice and her hands. "This man you call Reese . . . he is your father, Michael Stone." She turned away, both hands to her face. Grant froze in amazement, and then the pieces began to click into place as he relived what had happened from the time he had first blundered into the smugglers.

114

Reese—Stone—had known where he, Grant, lived. The vague, puzzling familiarity was explained now too, and why Grant's mother had been taken hostage so easily.

"Don't take it so big, Grant," Mike Stone said to him, a grin frozen on his face now. "It's a rough world we live in, and a man does what he has to do."

"He's trying to tell you he's hijacking that heroin, Grant, and not working with the authorities. At first he almost had me fooled too. I wanted to believe him. Oh, I wanted that so bad, Mike." She broke off again, and Grant turned to comfort her.

"Okay, okay. I don't need another sermon, Flo," Mike Stone said harshly. "We came to an end of the road a long time ago. I didn't ask for your help. Grant just happened to stumble onto the deal."

"And to find out what kind of man he had for a father," she said bitterly. "Why don't you go, Mike? Go and leave us alone."

"Don't worry," Stone said, his face softening again. "And I promise you'll never see me again. I always did want to travel, and now I'll have the money to do it with. Grant . . . I wish it could have been different, but . . ."

He held out his hand tentatively, and Grant felt the sickness churning inside him. For a long moment his father held his hand out, then he shrugged and dropped it. Stooping, he picked up the bag and moved toward the airplane.

"You're going to leave us here?" Grant asked.

"Under the circumstances, Grant," Stone said coldly, "I don't have much choice, do I? I'm sure you can—"

The radio in the BG cut him off. Grant bent toward the instrument panel to snap it off when the words registered.

"Reese, put down the bag and head south on foot," the voice said, and in his mind, Grant could see the bearded face of the doper who had tried to ram him earlier in the day.

Turning his head, he looked toward Mike Stone to see what he would do. For perhaps five seconds Stone halted, his head cocked to look up at the plane that had appeared over the valley. Then he began to run.

"Mike!" Grant's mother cried. "Mike, you'd better stop!"

Mike Stone was at the airplane now, dumping the bag into the cabin and hastily climbing in himself.

The radio crackled again. "Reese, don't be a fool. It was a good try, but you blew it. Leave the stuff where it is and walk south. We won't bother you."

Grant lost the rest in the racket of the starting engine. Almost immediately the Cessna swiveled on one wheel and began to roll back toward them. A hand waved as the wheels left the ground, and Mike Stone and his stolen fortune in heroin slanted up out of the valley.

But he was a few seconds too late. Grant's mother held tightly to his arm as they watched the higher aircraft begin its dive. As in a dream, Grant heard his mother cry, "Oh, no. Mike, Mike!"

From that distance he couldn't really hear the impact as the undercarriage of the higher plane tore into the tail surfaces of the one just leaving the ground, but he imagined he heard it. He could hear his own voice too, echoing his mother's cry as they watched the slow motion of tragedy fifty feet in the air.

He would never know whether the lower plane flipped upward because of the pilot's lack of control, or whether the pilot deliberately pulled up. The result was the same. Stone's craft caught the propeller of the attacking plane squarely in its wing center section. Trapped, the higher plane rolled nose down with its victim, and as Grant's mother screamed hysterically, both aircraft hit the ground. This time Grant could hear the crumpling noise clearly, even though he could believe none of what he was seeing. For an instant the

116

impression was like that of an old comic movie in which everything went wrong. Then, as the first flames spurted from the tumbling wreckage, Grant began to run numbly toward the crash.

His feet were like lead. When he was still twenty feet from the inferno, he knew he could not even reach it, much less do any good. With both arms flung up to shield himself from the fierce heat, he glimpsed the smashed cabin of one plane momentarily, and then shut his eyes and turned away. His mother was stumbling toward him, and he ran to stop her. Half dragging and half carrying her, he moved away to a safe distance and then held her tenderly, trying to shut out the nightmare of fire and explosions.

As soon as he could, Grant helped his mother to a spot upwind of the wreckage, away from the sickening stench that threatened to empty his stomach. She huddled against a rock, her head cradled in her arms, crying softly to herself. Then Grant went slowly back to the BG and found the microphone. His voice heavy, he made a call on the emergency frequency.

"Mayday! Mayday!" he cried, using the distress signal for the first time in his flying career. "This is Briegleb sailplane Eight-Eight-Hotel reporting a plane crash." The answer came quickly.

"Eight-Hotel, this is Williams Air Force Base. Go ahead."

Slowly, fighting a terrible sickness of body and spirit, Grant told the man what had happened and gave him their location. Then he shut off the radio and retraced his steps to where his mother was.

"It's all over, Mom," he told her, kneeling beside her and covering his eyes with a grimy hand. "I've called for help."

CHAPTER 10

A narcotics agent put it all together for Grant while a doctor worked on his legs. Mike Stone had been a bold and clever man. He had tried to reach his ex-wife at the field but had been put off by the phony mechanics swarming about. So he simply got on the phone and called her. Stunned to hear from her ex-husband after so long, and led on by his persuasive talk of having something that had to be settled, she told the agents she had to make a check flight in the Cessna and flew off to meet Stone at a little-used airport north of Tucson. From then on there was nothing she could do but comply with his demands and radio Grant to fly to Picnic Valley.

The agents were monitoring the radio, of course, and knew all that was happening, but they had no idea where Picnic Valley was. Word went out to the men guarding the secret strip originally set for the landing of the sailplane. But even with a plane searching the area, the agents were helpless until they heard Grant's Mayday call after it was all over.

Harry Shaughnessy, blasting along on the ground with the trailer, had heard the earlier call and had the mike in his hand, ready to put in his indignant nickel's worth, when he changed his mind and just drove like a madman to reach the rendezvous in time. The doper in the towplane, infuriated by Reese's obvious hijacking attempt, tried to knock Grant out of the sky. Failing that and unable to find Grant after the cloud episode, the man blundered onto the trailer, ahead of a cloud of dust far below. When he saw the big GS painted on top, it rang a bell, and the pilot flew down and forced Harry off the deserted dirt road. Harry, half unconscious from a bump on the head when he went into a dry wash, was forced to tell the pilot where Picnic Valley was, and the tragic confrontation was set up.

With the pressure of testimony from Grant, Harry, and his mother, the surviving smuggler talked enough about the big man in Los Angeles so the agents thought they would be able to nail him before long. At the very least, half a million dollars' worth of heroin and the uncountable cost in human tragedy that it could have led to were destroyed in the crash, although enough trace of the drug remained to establish its identity.

The days after the crash were terrible. The funeral came first, and Grant went only because he knew that his being there meant something to his mother. Harry went too, and that made a total of three on hand for the last rites of the man named Mike Stone—his father. He couldn't comprehend his mother's anguish. His own feelings were those of bitter disappointment, even disgust.

Not that Grant was glad his father had died in the flaming wreckage. Just the opposite was closer to his true feelings when he could sort them out. Mike Stone's death had been a stupid climax to the whole rotten, senseless business. Grant felt no relief that his father had been taken from the scene so conveniently, no gratitude that rough justice had been done for the man's terrible wrongs. The last episode simply deepened the soul sickness that had eaten at Grant for so long.

The narcotics people had tactfully delayed the questioning

session for Grant and his mother. Respect for the dead was the heading that must come under. But the day after Mike Stone was put under the ground, two polite officers arrived at the airport and drove Grant and his mother to Phoenix for an inquiry into the bizarre smuggling episode. It was perfectly understandable, Grant had to admit. He couldn't blame the agents for putting two and two together and getting four.

An ex–Air Force officer, a former resident of the state, had suddenly shown up in the area and become involved in a series of drug-smuggling operations. When he was killed in a crash seemingly engineered by men who were either his partners or hijack victims, Mike Stone had been in the company of his divorced wife and his son. And the son, by his own admission, had twice flown heroin from Mexico into Arizona.

It was a harrowing session. Grant was grilled first, and then his mother. Then both of them were interrogated by a battery of narcotics agents, attorneys general, and even FAA officials. The point was made that a sailplane contest had been used as a clever cover for the pickup of a large package of heroin, and Grant knew that the Soaring Club had been contacted. He could only imagine what they thought about the hotshot pilot who had won the first leg of the competition and then turned smuggler under that cover.

Had they not told the investigator about it earlier, Grant wondered how they would have fared. That admission, plus the testimony of Harry Shaughnessy and others, eventually put them in the clear.

"Well, Mrs. Stone, Grant," the Department of Public Safety captain finally told them one hot morning in his office in Phoenix. "We're satisfied that both of you were not criminally involved in any part of the operation. Sorry we had to be pretty rough at times, but this has been a sticky one."

120

"We understand," Florence Stone said, nodding. Grant noticed that her reaction seemed about the same as his. Surely they were relieved to be free, but there were no big smiles or glad cries of joy. They hadn't won anything, just avoided losing more.

"We are free to go?" Grant's mother asked.

"Yes, ma'am. I'm . . . sorry about Mr. Stone," the man said awkwardly. Then he put out his hand and it was over. At least that part of it was.

There were still stories in the papers. Grant learned not to read anything or to watch TV. Understandably, some reporters—and their readers—continued to believe that the smuggling ring had been a cozy family affair. Harry had done a fine job of keeping the airport going, but it was obvious that their business had fallen off. Who wanted to fly at "Smuggler's Field"?

Still, it eased the hurt a little to get home after the long days in Phoenix. Stone Field looked the same as ever, and Harry stayed for supper so he could fill them in on how things were going. Obviously he wanted to know the whole story. He had appeared twice with them in Phoenix, once as a witness, and again as a character reference.

"Just this one time," Grant's mother said. They were in the living room drinking coffee, and Grant's unwillingness to go through it again must have showed. "Please stay, Grant," his mother said. "Then it will be done. For good."

He stayed, and she talked slowly of the whole tragic affair, beginning with Mike Stone's deserting her and Grant so long ago.

"It's funny I didn't suspect it could be Mike when you described Joe Reese," she said, looking at Grant. "But I really didn't, even when he called that day you were flying in the contest. Before I got over the shock, I was a prisoner. A hostage he called it."

121

Mike Stone had told her that involving Grant in the smuggling was an accident. Mike had come back to the Southwest when he was offered a chance to make some big money flying drugs across the border. He had fought it off for a long time, but he was deep in debt and in other trouble in the East, where he had lived for years, so he finally gave in and came to Arizona. He carefully kept away from Stone Field for obvious reasons. Then Grant had blundered into the operation.

Mike's story was that when the other two heard Grant was his son, they put terrible pressure on him to get the boy into the deal. Which may or may not have been true. Grant couldn't believe—he would never believe—that Mike was anything but a greedy hijacker, who saw a chance to get all the proceeds from the last big deal, instead of sharing them with the two other men.

Oddly, Mike Stone *had* worked as an informer twice before, but the card he had shown Grant as an agent's ID was nothing more than his old Air Force card.

Mike Stone had been a personable man and an excellent pilot. Why he couldn't settle for that and live an honest life was a mystery to Grant, but he couldn't. Stone had been a loner and a bad apple. He had boasted to his former wife that he had never been involved in physical violence, and to Grant, this seemed ironic, because heroin addiction was about as hellish a harm as could be piled on a victim. Grant's only consolation was that the drugs had been confiscated and destroyed. At least that many kilos of heroin would not wreck more lives.

Slowly they began to pick up the broken pieces and got to work putting them back together. With business off, it was possible to catch up on things that had once been allowed to slide by. Grant worked automatically, like a robot programmed to do what needed doing, without knowing or caring what he did. It showed on his face and in his eyes, and his mother misread what she saw there.

"It's hard, Grant," she told him one day, putting an arm around his shoulders. "But business will get better. People will forget or think better of things. And—"

"Mom, I don't care what people think or forget," he exploded. "You think I'm just worried that we might not make money with the airport? We could get rich, and I'd still feel the way I do now!"

"And how is that?" she asked, moving away from him. He noticed that the creases above her soft eyes made her look older.

"Dead," he said bitterly. "I feel dead inside. What have I got left? I'm ashamed to pick up a paper or watch the TV news. I'm afraid I'll meet somebody who knows me. Grant Stone, the junkie sailplane pilot!"

"Grant, please," she began, but he turned and fled.

He ran to the pickup, climbed into it, and drove off. The sun had gone down when he came back. His mother had the table set, and he could smell food in the kitchen. Ashamed, he washed up and came to the table. She said grace and they ate silently for several minutes.

"May I say one thing?" she asked finally.

He looked up and nodded. "Sure, Mom. I'm sorry I shot off my mouth."

"I know, dear. Believe me, I know. But life goes on, Grant. Bitter as we may be, life goes on. With us or without us. And bitter as you may be, you have life. Think about that. And who gave you that life, Grant? Your father disappointed you terribly, but he gave you that much."

Grant shook his head slightly, not understanding what she was saying.

"Besides life itself, he gave you your love of flying, Grant.

123

Never forget that gift. And never forget the responsibility it carries."

"Mom!" he protested.

"Lecture over," she said abruptly, smiling through the tears that had started. "Think about it, Grant, that's all I ask. Now how about some pie?"

There was no sudden revelation; there were no sudden peals of happy organ music. He moped and scowled for a long time, and sometimes the mood would hit him to take the truck and head for the hills. But the day came when he caught himself whistling again. The next day he went to church for the first time in a long time. Then one Saturday morning he flew the Citabria, and it wasn't all bad.

The day came when he cut the throttle of the Citabria under a huge cumulus cloud and thrilled again as he rode upward on a strong lift. That part of him still lived, so much that it hurt to leave the rising current of air and start the plane's engine.

And at last, in the fall, there came a time when he went to the long trailer gathering dust along the hangar wall. He had the heart now to open the door and look again at the broken bird inside. And he was able to tell himself that his mother was right. Somehow he would put the BG back together so it could soar again. With him at the controls.